DEATH ON A DARK NIGHT

Myra Wahl turned off from the bustling traffic of Pico Boulevard to the dark streets of Gateway. She was feeling calmer now. Running always did that to her.

The hum of an approaching automobile interrupted her thoughts. She swung around and jogged backwards a few paces. In the distance all she could see was the approaching lights of a large car. She turned back and resumed her normal strides. A few seconds later she twisted around again. The noise of the engine sounded much closer than it should have. Pedaling backwards she moved toward the sidewalk. But the brights were now on, blinding her. Instinctively she looked down. The wheels of the car were turning, turning—they were coming directly at her. She moved faster—but not fast enough. . . .

At six-thirty A.M., the phone rang beside the bed of Daniel Winter. He checked his watch, groaned, then picked up the receiver. The rabbi did not know it at the time, but he was about to become a detective.

THE UNORTHODOX MURDER
OF RABBI WAHL

The First Case for
Los Angeles Rabbi Daniel Winter

THE UNORTHODOX MURDER OF RABBI WAHL

Joseph Telushkin

5/19/87

L'Chayim,

Joseph Telushkin

BANTAM BOOKS
TORONTO · NEW YORK · LONDON · SYDNEY · AUCKLAND

THE UNORTHODOX MURDER OF RABBI WAHL
A Bantam Book / May 1987

ISBN 0-553-25809-5

Published simultaneously in the United States and Canada

Bantam Books are published by Bantam Books, Inc. Its trademark,
consisting of the words "Bantam Books" and the portrayal of a
rooster, is Registered in U.S. Patent and Trademark Office and in
other countries. Marca Registrada. Bantam Books, Inc., 666 Fifth
Avenue, New York, New York 10103.

PRINTED IN THE UNITED STATES OF AMERICA

0 9 8 7 6 5 4 3 2 1

Acknowledgments

Several friends read this book while in manuscript and gave me both encouragement and, even more importantly, concrete suggestions for improvement. I'm happy to have this chance to thank them, and request forgiveness from anyone whose name I have inadvertantly omitted: David Brandes, Debra Friedland, Michael Gillis and Angela Rosen, Dore and Ofra Gold, Linda Kaplan, Harvey Mayerson, Hillel Riskin, Alex Singer, Levi and Paula Weiman-Kelman, and a very special thanks to Daniel Taub. I also had occassion to incorporate (though in a considerably transformed state) an anecdote I heard from the great Jerusalem Bible scholar and teacher, Nechama Leibowitz.

Linda Kachani worked with me over a period of several months, and her suggestions and emendations touch every page of this book. I feel truly blessed to have had her assistance.

I am particularly pleased to express my gratitude to Richard Pine, my agent, whose initial enthusiasm so encouraged me. And at Bantam I'd like to thank Nessa Rappaport, and my own editor, Kate Miciak, whose stylistic and editorial suggestions were, quite simply, brilliant.

Monday

Rabbi Daniel Winter nibbled on his pen, flipped through his third-class mail, crumpled papers into balls, aimed them at the wastepaper basket, and stared at the sheet in front of him. After forty-five minutes, it contained one line, "Counting Time or Making Time Count." He desperately longed to crumple that paper, too, and write an entirely different sermon. But the title had gone out in the synagogue bulletin, and if he spoke on a different subject he could already hear Wilbur Kantor, the synagogue's president, make his usual wry comment. "Rabbi, in the construction business when I tell someone I'm going to do a job, I do it. And I do the job I promised to do. Is it too much to ask that you do the same?"

It would be yet another pointless victory for Kantor in their permanent undeclared war. Without enthusiasm, Daniel returned to the paper. He had no more delaying tactics left.

Salvation came a moment later in the form of Pat Hastings, his secretary. She knocked once and walked in. Slim and blond, Pat looked considerably younger than her forty-five years.

"Have you been doing something naughty, Rabbi?"

Daniel grinned. Pat rarely called him "Rabbi" except when she was teasing.

She said, "There is a *Ms*. Brenda Goldstein to see you. No appointment. I told her that these were your study hours and you couldn't be disturbed. She insisted it was important, that she was from the police department, homicide division."

"Homicide?" the rabbi mused. "Nothing's happened to Wilbur, I hope?"

1

"You're impossible," Pat laughed. "What do I tell Ms. Goldstein?"

"Send her in. She definitely sounds more interesting than my sermon."

She was.

Brenda Goldstein was tall, with long red hair, a sprinkling of freckles, light green eyes, and no ring on her left hand. She moved easily into the vacant armchair in front of Daniel's desk and met his gaze with an air of crisp determination.

"Is this police business, Ms. Goldstein?"

"Not exactly." She hesitated, then added bluntly, "But it got me in to see you."

They both laughed. What an advantage pretty women had, he thought. If an unattractive woman had done the same thing, he would have been annoyed with her. And then with himself for being annoyed. He had long since despaired of understanding why a God who loved mankind had made some of them so unattractive.

"Actually, I'm not here on homicide business. But it is something that could concern the police." She paused for a moment, a furrow between her brows. "You don't know who I am, do you?"

"I hope you're not a member here."

Brenda nodded, half smiling.

"And I never noticed you before?"

"I'm a three-day-a-year Jew. When I'm here, it's with a thousand other people. I joined for my daughter's sake. Jessica is in the congregation's bar and bat mitzvah class," Brenda said.

He stared at her in amazement.

"I know what you're thinking. I had her when I was nineteen. Five years ago I got divorced. Last year I decided that if I can't give Jessie a traditional two-parent home, at least I can give her something traditional. So I joined."

"Why this congregation?"

"A friend gave me your book, *The Religious Manifesto*. It made quite an impression on me."

"But not enough to get you to come here more than three days a year?"

"Touché, Rabbi. Someday I'll tell you about my quarrel

with God. In the meantime, *we* have a more pressing problem." Daniel's eyebrows lifted at the unexpected pronoun. "You have a twelve-year-old thief in your bar mitzvah class."

"What!"

"This past weekend, the class went away to the synagogue camp. Unknown to me, Jessica took with her the one valuable piece of jewelry I own: a gold watch with inlaid diamonds that was passed down to me from my grandmother. Rabbi, that watch is valued at fifteen hundred dollars. But to me, it's worth much more. Three years after she gave it to my mother, my grandmother was murdered at Auschwitz. That watch is the only link I have left with her. I've told Jessica the story of that watch many times. Apparently she wanted to impress the other kids with it. Saturday night she took it out, showed it off, and passed it around. It made a very big impression on at least one person. Sometime that night or the next morning the watch was stolen."

"I'm terribly sorry, Ms. Goldstein. I'm also extraordinarily embarrassed. But I don't understand. Today is Monday. Why didn't I hear about this yesterday?"

"Because Jessica didn't realize the watch was stolen until last night. After showing it around, she put it back in her bag and didn't check for it again. Until she got home. That's when all hell broke loose. She became hysterical. It took me a long time to calm her down and when I finally understood what was missing, *I* became hysterical. I'm calmer now, Rabbi. But if I don't get that watch back soon. . . ." Her eyes glittered.

"I understand," Daniel said, "but are you positive it was one of our students who took it?"

"No question, Rabbi." She met his eyes squarely. "First, nobody else knew about the watch but the children to whom Jessie showed it. Second, you know that campsite far better than I. It was locked up tight Saturday night. The only other possibility is that someone climbed the fence, sneaked into Jessie's cabin, and removed the one item from her overnight bag that had any value. Rabbi, I've spoken with the other girls in the cabin. Nothing else was stolen but that watch. It was definitely taken by someone who was there for the weekend, someone who knew where Jessie had put it."

"What do you need me to do, Ms. Goldstein?"

"You don't have to do anything. Just let some of my friends from the police department come here and investigate."

He frowned. "A police investigation? *Here* in the bar mitzvah class?"

"It will be rather routine, Rabbi. An officer will explain what happened, that we're dealing with grand larceny. He'll tell the children that if we don't get the watch back right away, he'll have to take fingerprints and check them against the prints on Jessie's bag. He'll mention that he might have to ask some people to take lie detector tests. Don't worry, Rabbi. With these kids' parents and their parents' lawyers, none of these things will come to pass. But I do predict it will put the fear of God into someone. We can have the whole thing cleared up in a couple of hours."

"If by cleared up, you mean you'll have your watch back, you might be right. But do you have any idea of the traumas you might unleash? Twelve-year-olds threatened with fingerprints, lie detector tests?"

"Don't worry about the trauma. I know something about that; I'm a psychologist in the police department. I admit it won't be pleasant. But I want that watch back. Now, are you going to help me?"

The rabbi stared past Brenda Goldstein. He picked up a pen, and absentmindedly chewed on it, his blue eyes focused on a distant point. A minute passed.

"Rabbi?"

A slight inclination of the young rabbi's head indicated that he had heard her, though barely. Then with a quick movement he rose from his desk, moved to the door, and held it open.

"I will help you, but in a different way. Without fingerprints and lie detectors. The class meets this afternoon at four. Please be there."

"Dammit, Rabbi—" she flared.

"Ms. Goldstein, what you see as a police matter, I see first of all as a religious matter. Be here at four."

* * *

For the second time that month, Bonnie Shanker was in shock. A short, mousy young woman, this was her first teaching job, and she wasn't enjoying it one bit. Two weeks earlier she had administered a straw poll at Rabbi Winter's request. She had asked the class: "If you saw your dog and a stranger, both drowning, and you could only save one, which one would you save?" Forty percent of her students said they would save their dog. Another forty percent were uncertain whom they would save. She had argued with the dog lovers for two sessions, but with little success.

"I *love* my dog. I don't love the stranger," said Robin Falk with inscrutable logic, while others nodded in agreement. When Miss Shanker had begun, rather desperately, to speak of "man's creation in God's image," she met with blank stares. Now she had learned that one of her students had stolen a watch worth over fifteen hundred dollars. She was relieved that the rabbi had insisted upon teaching the class today. If she had to do it, she didn't know what she would say.

At precisely four o'clock, the rabbi, followed by Brenda Goldstein, strode into the noisy classroom. The students already knew, via the grapevine, why Rabbi Winter was here, and their reactions were mixed. Gary Rosenstein, who looked forward to his bar mitzvah only for the computer his father had promised him, thought it was the first interesting thing that had happened in Hebrew school in two years. He was excited to see someone from the police department, even though she was only a woman and only Jessica Goldstein's mother. This was as good as the movies. Anne Rodman was terrified. She had nothing to do with the stolen watch, but in her purse was a vanity mirror for which Woolworth's had never received payment. And sitting in the last seat of the third row was one student, both anxious and excited, who faintly regretted stealing the watch, but was certain there was no reason to fear discovery.

When twelve-year-old Donna Gillis darted in at 4:05 and slithered guiltily into her seat, Bonnie Shanker indicated with a nod to the rabbi that everyone was present. Daniel stepped in front of her desk and sat down on its edge. The murmuring stopped as he looked straight into the eyes of first one student, then another. Then, in a deceptively mild voice, he began.

"I understand from Ms. Shanker that you all know why I am here. So I won't waste time on preliminaries.

"There are twenty-four people in this room, but I am speaking to only one of you—the one who stole Jessica Goldstein's watch. I have a few thoughts I want to share with you. Officer Goldstein of the police department tells me that this robbery is grand larceny. But I have other news which might make you happy. It is very unlikely that you will be caught." Daniel didn't miss the look of annoyance that flickered on Brenda Goldstein's face.

"I've spent the afternoon looking at statistics and have learned that the percentage of robberies actually solved is very small. So you have committed a robbery, maybe your first, and probably gotten away with it.

"But one thing I promise you. It will not be your last. For you have found out that it is easy to steal. And as you continue to steal, it will become even easier. You will find that you will have more money and more luxuries than your friends. In many ways you will have an easier life than the people around you who work for their money. You will have only one disadvantage—you will always have to live with the knowledge that you are a thief. Other people can take pride in what they have earned and what they own. But you will always know that what you possess you haven't earned. And even so, you will continue to steal because you will be used to getting things without working. And you will not be able to stop."

The rabbi paused. The only sound in the room was the ticking of the large clock above the classroom door.

"There is only one hope for you, and listen to me very carefully, because this is your one chance *not* to be a thief for the rest of your life. Return the watch. On Wednesday, you all come back here for class. At some point before then, put the watch in a public place where it will be found. So far you have committed one robbery. *If* you return the watch you become an honest person again. Tell no one what you have done. Don't tell your friends, your parents, or me. No one need ever know. And you need never steal again. You will have as clean a record as anyone else. You will be an honest person. *But if you don't return the watch* there is no going back. You will always have to live with the knowledge that you are a thief. *But if* you return it"—Daniel's voice started to rise—"you will be happy, I will be happy, the Goldstein family will be happy, and your whole future will be given back to you."

The rabbi stopped speaking, took a last look around the class, and walked quickly out of the room, shutting the door hard. Brenda Goldstein followed almost immediately.

"Do you think it will work?" she asked, struggling to keep up with the rabbi's angry strides, her heels clicking on the floor behind him.

"What do you think?"

"Personally, I don't think you did the right thing, Rabbi. When you're dealing with a thief, whether he's twelve or fifty, you have to scare him. You have to talk about punishment." When the rabbi didn't respond, she added, "Perhaps I have less faith in human nature than you do."

They were standing now in front of the rabbi's study. He looked at Brenda, his face grave.

"That's not the difference between us. You want to catch the thief so that you can get your watch back. I want your watch back, but I don't want to catch the thief. I want to stop someone from becoming a thief." He paused. "Don't you think everyone is entitled to a second chance?"

Brenda Goldstein bristled. Her green eyes flashed.

"Don't play rabbi games with me. What am I supposed to say, that someone is not entitled to a second chance? What I want to know is what we do Thursday after the watch is not returned."

"*If* the watch is not returned," said Daniel, and he entered his study and closed the door, leaving Brenda glaring at the empty space where he had been standing.

Wednesday

Shortly before six o'clock, Luther Johnson, the synagogue janitor, tapped on the door and entered the rabbi's study, a triumphant smile on his face. He stretched out a broad fist, then opened it. Daniel gasped. Inside was a gold watch. Luther placed it carefully on the rabbi's desk. "It was on the ledge in front of the Torah ark. Mazal tov, Rabbi."

The rabbi grinned at his use of the Hebrew term and went straight to his cabinet and pulled out a bottle of Johnnie Walker and two shot glasses. He poured out both glasses, his blue eyes bright with exultation.

"This calls for a celebration, Luther."

Luther Johnson downed the whiskey smoothly in one long gulp. In macho style the rabbi matched him. And then started to cough. And cough. Luther Johnson laughed heartily, slapping his sides.

"If I ever want to learn Torah, I'll ask you to teach me. If you ever want to learn how to drink, Rabbi, I'll teach you."

The rabbi's sputters turned to laughter.

"Luther, if you keep calling me Rabbi, I'll have to call you Mr. Johnson. So why don't you call me Daniel?"

"You know what, Rabbi? I've worked at this congregation for twenty-two years. You're the fifth rabbi I've worked for. And you know something? Outside of the bookkeeper, you're the first person in this whole building who ever learned my last name. I like that. It's just fine with me if you call me Mister Johnson. It sounds good."

The rabbi refilled Johnson's glass and raised his own. "Mr. Johnson, I can't thank you enough for finding this watch."

8

Luther Johnson grinned, finished his drink, and waved good-bye.

The rabbi picked up the watch. Brenda Goldstein had not exaggerated its beauty. Its dial was gold, and a fine layer of diamonds bordered the edges. The figures, in black numerals, were set in delicate oval disks. Holding it to the light of his desk lamp, he turned it over and peered at the Hebrew inscription on the back. It was very faint and took several minutes to decipher. "For Esther from Moshe Leib," he read, and then saw the verse from the Song of Songs: "For love is as strong as death." Instantly, he thought of his wife, Rebecca, dead these three years. She had been only twenty-nine when the doctors told them she had cancer. His eyes misted. He looked around his dark, cluttered office and was engulfed by a feeling of emptiness. He remembered how, when he had first realized that Rebecca's illness was not going to be cured, he had felt glad they had no children. The responsibility would have been overwhelming. But as she grew weaker, the lack of a child began to obsess him. Nothing would remain, no living evidence that they had loved. Nothing except this yearning, now familiar, for the gentle girl who had been his closest companion. "For love is as strong as death," he murmured. He thought of the murdered Esther, then of the dead Moshe Leib. What was left now of Esther—a watch, an inscription, and a granddaughter, Brenda Goldstein, who he was sure could not read the Hebrew inscription.

The phone rang. He ignored it. His answering machine picked it up on the third ring. Absently, he heard his own voice drone its seemingly interminable message. And then he heard Brenda Goldstein. "Rabbi, Jessica came home from school and told me the watch has not been returned. If I offended you the other day, I'm sorry, very sorry. But I must have that watch back. What do you intend to do now?" A pause, then, "Please call."

The last words were said with a vulnerability he had not heard in her before, and he was suddenly out of his melancholy. He pulled out the synagogue membership list and found the Goldstein address. Brenda Goldstein was about to learn that rabbis were among the rare professionals who still made house calls.

As Daniel stood in front of the house on the 300 block of Dalehurst, in Westwood, a sense of déjà vu assailed him. What was so familiar about this place? It was an elegantly built gray house with an air of classical grandeur, standing in an immense stretch of lawn with a small fountain in the center, surrounded by a circular plot of chrysanthemums. This house was not supported on a police psychologist's salary. He pulled on the large block knocker and smiled to see the mezuzah on the doorpost.

When Brenda Goldstein opened the door, tall and severe in black, she met with a beaming Rabbi Winter holding the missing watch out in his right hand. With an audible gasp, she snatched it from his hand, then impulsively threw her arms around him. Immediately she drew back. "Oh, I'm so sorry, Rabbi!"

"I'm not," Daniel smiled, and invited himself in.

"Wait here, Rabbi," Brenda said, taking his blue jacket. "I'm going to phone Jessica. She'll be so happy."

Daniel stepped into the light-filled living room. The tables, chairs, and cabinets were all of the same dark ivory, and there was a long white couch at the back of the room. The effect was at once cozy and antique. He was impressed, even a little awed. Brenda Goldstein was clearly a woman of taste. He wondered how she would react to the lopsided pile of magazines, the misplaced books, and the uncleaned dishes in his own house. Then he thought how he would clean it up before he brought her there. It was odd. At his office he had found her attractive, but that had been an objective, uninvolved reaction. Now his mind was already planning future encounters. A voice inside him pulled him back to earth. What could he be thinking of? Brenda was not of his world—she was not religious. Besides, she was a member of his congregation.

Brenda returned, interrupting his confused thoughts.

"Rabbi, Jessica came home from school so upset that I let her go over to Donna Gillis'. She's just told me that she wants to sleep there. So I'm stuck with a lot of extra spaghetti and meatballs. Could I interest you?"

"You do interest me," Daniel said. "But unfortunately, I have a sneaking suspicion that the meatballs aren't kosher."

Brenda reddened and Daniel hurried on. "But this looks pretty good."

He sat down on the couch and helped himself from the large bowl of fruit on the oval glass table in front of him. Then he turned and beamed up at her. Laughing, she took a seat opposite him.

"You know, Ms. Goldstein—"

"Rabbi," she interrupted, "please call me Brenda."

"Only if you call me Daniel."

"I couldn't call a rabbi by his first name."

"Why not?"

"It's seems so disrespectful."

"To whom?"

Brenda was silent.

"When I got the title "Rabbi," it became my first name. It's easy for everyone. They never have to remember my name. Worse, people don't act naturally when I'm around. I'll be in a group and somebody will use a four-letter word and then stammer, 'Oh, excuse me, Rabbi.' It drives me crazy. I have to laugh at inane jokes just to convince people that I'm not a pompous ass. Aside from my secretary—and with her it was a struggle—the only people who call me by my first name are other rabbis."

"Okay, okay, you've convinced me, Daniel. By the way, I owe you an apology. I didn't think you knew what you were talking about in your little speech to the class. I suppose I was even a bit rude. But you got the watch back. Congratulations."

"And I'm sorry I slammed my office door in your face."

They looked at each other and laughed. Daniel leaned back on the soft white-cushioned sofa, still chewing on his apple, and drew a long breath. He had not laughed like this with a woman in a long time. He thought how pretty the golden freckles were around her eyes. "So tell me," he asked, "how did you get into the police department?" Brenda told him that she had a Ph.D. in clinical psychology, but had grown impatient with a practice that restricted her to treating a maximum of twenty people. Her current job with the police department was an experimental one. She was assigned to the homicide division, specializing in murders of women.

This big house was the one she had grown up in. "My parents lived here until they . . . died two years ago."

Daniel remembered the sense of familiarity he had felt on first seeing the house. Suddenly, his mouth went dry.

"Your parents were murdered, weren't they?"

Brenda bit hard on her lip and turned aside, avoiding his eyes. He barely caught her nod.

"Jean and Ted Kaplan," Daniel said slowly. "My God. It happened a few weeks after I became rabbi here." And then in a subdued voice, he asked, "They were killed in this house, weren't they?"

"Yes."

"I came here that week, during shiva. I met your parents' brothers and sisters. They told me there was one child, but she couldn't be located. Where were you?"

"I was incommunicado," Brenda began, the words coming out hesitantly. "Jessica and I were traveling in Italy and France, and I didn't know where we would be from day to day. I'd call my parents every ten days or so. I spoke to them the night before they died. The next time I called, the week of mourning was finished and my Aunt Ruth had closed up the house. When I got no answer after three days of calling, I phoned her and found out what happened."

They sat quietly. Outside, a car screeched to a halt and then straightened and moved on.

"I came back to LA right away," Brenda continued. She had gained control of her voice, but her green eyes were dark with an old rage. "But after a few weeks, I returned to New York. I thought I could get on with my life, but nothing seemed to click. That's when I started feeling futile treating so few people. A friend sent me a notice about the opening out here for a police department psychologist. I called up, and a week later I was back in Los Angeles. Thank God the house hadn't been sold."

"Was the murderer caught?"

"Not yet."

"So that's also part of your agenda?"

"You're not stupid, Daniel. Yes, whenever a murder occurs in Los Angeles I check all the data, the ballistics, that sort of stuff, against my parents' case."

"And so far?"

Brenda brought her thumb and forefinger together to form a zero.

"Have the police given up?"

"Officially, they never close a homicide. Unofficially, yes. There's so little to go on. We can only surmise what happened." Her voice had become expressionless. "Apparently, a thief broke into the house while my parents were out. He was after my mother's jewelry; there was a lot of it. My parents must have come home and interrupted him. Knowing my father, I can see him trying to fight with the guy. But he didn't have a chance. They were both shot dead. Mercifully, they died immediately. Exactly two years next Wednesday, and we still don't have a lead. That gun hasn't been used in any other crimes we know of. We haven't found a trace of Mom's jewelry." Very gently, she picked up the watch Daniel had just returned. "She gave me this just a few months before she died. Now it's the only piece that's left."

For a moment, the room was quiet.

"Two years," she repeated. "I know time heals. But the healing is so slow. Maybe it's because they died so unexpectedly that I never had the chance to adjust. I don't know. Maybe it's because I caused them so much pain when Raymond and I divorced. They couldn't hide their hurt, and that made me furious. I loved them, but during those last years they didn't see much of my love. Just my anger. I loved them and I can tell you about it, but I can never say it to them."

Daniel studied her face, his eyes earnest as they looked into hers.

"You just did."

"What do you mean?"

"I believe they heard every word you just told me."

"You believe that?"

He nodded.

"Tell me the truth. Do you believe that all the time?"

"Yes," he said, and then remembered the melancholy he had felt earlier in the evening. But he was not Daniel now, he was Rabbi. She needed to hear his strength, he thought, not share in his occasional moods of despair.

"You're a remarkable man, Danniel. Or a remarkable liar."

At that moment it occurred to him that here was a woman he could come to care about a great deal. Already he regretted the lie he had told her. Of course he had doubts. A faith without doubts would be the deadest of faiths, the faith of a person who had no expectations from God. Someday, he knew, he would tell her this. But not now.

Now, all he wanted was to lift that wretchedness from her eyes. With a deftness born of long experience, he brought the conversation back to her career. Gradually, she began to smile again and started to draw him out. He told her about Luther Johnson, the board, Pat Hastings, his work. And when finally he got up to leave, it seemed utterly natural to say, "When do I see you again?"

"Sunday evening's good for me."

"But I do my radio show Sunday night."

"Radio show? Hey, Rabbi—excuse me, Daniel—you are a double threat! A rabbi and an entertainer!"

Daniel smiled self-consciously. "Actually, it's a religious show, *Religion and You*. Every week we have a guest minister, a priest, and a rabbi. People call up with personal questions, and I moderate the discussion."

"But how can you moderate? You're a rabbi yourself!"

"KLAX needed a host who knew something about religion, and fortunately my book was *The Religious Manifesto*, not *The Jewish Manifesto*. On the air I'm Mr. Daniel Winter, not 'Rabbi.'" He hesitated. He wanted very much to take her to the show. But it seemed an odd choice for a first date. On the other hand, the idea appealed to him. "Would you like to come?"

"Very much."

"It'll be good to have a cop there. This Sunday's show might get violent."

"Religion and You?" Brenda teased.

"This week's three clergy are all women—a rabbi, a minister, and a nun—and the topic for the evening is 'Feminism, Women and Religion.'"

"That's old hat by now. What's going to make it so controversial?"

"Rabbi Myra Wahl, for one. She's the assistant rabbi at the Pico Boulevard Temple and an aggressive feminist. She is also no fan of mine."

"How could anybody dislike you?"

He grimaced. "I'm not sure if that's a compliment, or if it just makes me sound pathetic. But anyway, you might recall a chapter in my book on the differences between men and women and the implications of those differences for religion. Myra Wahl has still not forgiven me for that chapter. As a matter of fact, when I invited her for Sunday she informed me that she intended to destroy me on the air."

"So why not disinvite her?"

"I suppose because I think it's good sometimes for people to see that religion deals with exciting issues. Also," and his grin was sheepish, "I think in a debate I'll destroy her before she destroys me."

"Who are the other panelists?"

"Reverend Joanne Short. She works with Protestant students at the University of the Southlands. Her politics are about two percent less radical than Myra's."

"And the nun?"

"Sister Mary Kuluski. I just pray she and I get along."

"Tell me, Daniel, are you a male chauvinist?"

He hesitated. "Probably I am. But sometimes I'm ashamed of it. . . . Are you a feminist?"

"Probably I am," she said gently, mimicking him. "But, then again, not all the time."

They looked at each other, relieved. "So how tough do you think it will get, Daniel? Should I bring my thirty-eight?"

They both laughed. Later they were to remember that laughter.

Sunday

Rabbi Myra Wahl made herself a tuna fish sandwich, took a bite, and spat it out. The tuna was fine. She wasn't. That morning the executive committee of the Pico Boulevard Temple had made it emphatic that they wanted her to resign now, a year before her contract as assistant rabbi expired. Her mind reverted with disgust to the scene in the temple conference room. "There's no point in fooling ourselves, Rabbi," Irv Burnside, synagogue treasurer, had said, shaking his bald head. "You're not what we want, and I suppose we're not what you want. We were one of the first Reform temples in this area to hire a woman rabbi. But we hired you to be a rabbi, not a resident feminist."

"And what's wrong with my being a feminist?" said Myra sharply. "You can't whitewash all your sins just by hiring me. You all know this synagogue is singularly unliberated. Just look around this room. Seven men. No women. It's time this synagogue had women on the executive committee, maybe even a woman president. I know I've said this often enough, but I'm going to keep pushing this issue."

"Rabbi," said Peter Adelman, in the voice normally reserved for his courtroom appearances. He pulled out a sheet of paper from the file in front of him and waved it gently. "I refer you again to the resolution which we passed just a year ago and which you accepted: 'The rabbis shall engage in no behavior which can be construed as political lobbying inside the congregation.'"

"This isn't politics. This is *justice*. What do you expect a rabbi to speak about?"

16

She looked for support to Reuben Rappaport, the senior rabbi, who in the past had always had a pleasant word for her. But she couldn't catch his eye; he was suddenly preoccupied with some papers in front of him.

"Rabbi," said Brian Levin, immaculately dressed, his deep voice almost thundering. "The women's stuff is only one of many issues. You're just too damn *angry*. How do you think that I felt, as chairman of the UJA campaign, when you declared in a sermon that the only country in which Reform Jews have fewer rights than Israel is the Soviet Union, and followed it with an appeal for people to consider withholding their contributions?"

"I don't retract what I said."

"Well, you should have!" Rabbi Rappaport broke in, and with such force that Myra Wahl finally realized how alone she was.

Milton Karp, the synagogue's president, spoke last. A balding man with an aquiline nose and thin lips, his small gray eyes blinked compulsively as he surveyed the people seated around the table. "Rabbi—Myra, if I may—I know you believe that your problems here are the result of a personal vendetta on my part. I hope it's clear to you by now that this feeling of disappointment extends far beyond my own. For your sake, for our sake, let us recognize this fact and act accordingly."

Myra Wahl looked around the long, narrow table. "I just want to know one thing. Do you all agree with Milton?" It was funny, she thought, that she could hate someone so much and still call him by his first name.

One by one, she turned to them. Ron Cohen looked down, but nodded. Irv Burnside unflinchingly returned Myra's hard stare and said yes. Gene Stemkin looked at her, too, and said, "I'm sorry, Rabbi." Adelman just nodded. She looked at the senior rabbi. As an employee of the synagogue, Rappaport was not a member of the executive committee. Nonetheless, he spoke. An elderly, clean-shaven man, his voice had a faint German intonation. His usual pleasant smile was missing. "Myra, you had no stronger supporter in this congregation than me. But it's not working. I'm very sorry." The last two members said yes, and Myra turned to Karp with eyes so narrowed they were almost shut. "Well, you have the executive committee votes, Milton. But I think in an all-out war in the congregation I can beat you. And I'm no pacifist."

After the meeting adjourned, the members quickly dispersed, and Myra went straight over to Karp. She waited until they were alone in the room.

"You hate my guts, Milton. We both know that. I suppose you're happy now. It took you a year and a half to engineer this."

Milton Karp raised a thin gray eyebrow.

"Why should I hate you, Rabbi?"

"Because your daughter Janet feels more loyalty to me than to you. She's told me a lot about you." Her voice was scalding. "Does anybody else who was here today know that in Chicago, thirty, or to be precise, thirty-two years ago, you went to prison for stock manipulation? Or am I one of the chosen few who knows that you're a convicted felon?"

"What are you planning, Rabbi?," he asked very quietly, but she noted that the fingers holding the briefcase tightened on the handle.

"Oh, I don't know," Myra shrugged, "but I think the congregation has the right to know about the character of its president."

Milton Karp spoke deliberately, his face ashen.

"Watch your step, little girl. I think you ought to leave this job now, while you're still in good health." He nodded, a frozen smile on his lips, and left.

Furious, Myra followed him into the synagogue hallway. A woman's figure was walking swiftly, almost running, around the corner, and Karp hurried after it. But by the time Myra rounded the corner, both Milton Karp and the woman were gone. All Myra saw was the heavy iron exit door slowly shutting.

Brenda Goldstein set down her two bags of groceries, ran to the phone, and managed to get it on its fifth ring.

"It's Daniel. The synagogue is a madhouse this afternoon—it's our annual parent-teacher—"

"I hope you're not calling to cancel our date."

"Cancel? God forbid. I just won't be able to pick you up first for dinner." Brenda was quiet. "Hey, police lady, you caught me off guard. I had a whole speech planned about what a crazy day I was having. . . . Are you still there?"

"Yes," she said, laughter bubbling in her voice.

"Well, do you grant me my postponement?"

"Only if we go out for dinner after the program."

"That's not fair. That was *my* closing line."

They both laughed, each relieved to know the other one cared.

"I'll meet you at the KLAX parking lot at eight-thirty."

Two hours to the radio show. Earlier in the week, Myra had carefully worked out her line of attack against Daniel Winter's book. Now, as she reviewed it, she couldn't concentrate; the hostility of the executive committee had deeply shaken her. She had known they didn't like her. Of course not, she thought. They hated her because she had the guts to confront them with their hypocrisies. But it had never occurred to her that they would force her to resign.

Putting *The Religious Manifesto* aside impatiently, she stared at the mirror above her desk. She shook her head. No. No. No. She was a reasonably attractive woman, with her long, light brown hair, clear skin, and lithe athletic physique—the result of a careful regime of tennis three times a week and a daily five-mile jog. So why was it that at this moment all she could see in the mirror was a loser? She wanted to cry, but she wouldn't let herself. That's just what Milton Karp would want. Until now she had lived her life in defiance of the Milton Karps of the world. She couldn't stop now. Besides, she thought with satisfaction, she had hurt Karp just as deeply as he had hurt her.

Eighteen months before, Janet Karp had come to her for counseling, profoundly ambivalent about a father who had given her everything she had ever asked for, except a feeling of self-worth. It hadn't taken long for Myra to comprehend the dynamics of the father-daughter relationship. Milton Karp could be an extremely generous man, but only to those who gave him control over their lives in return. For twenty-four years, Janet Karp had done just that. The result was that although she was rich, pretty, and bright, she saw herself as a failure and had been institutionalized once for depression. After releasing her, the doctors had kept her on antidepressants, but Myra was convinced that Janet's depression was not simply biological. With her help Janet had come to understand where the real source of her depression lay. Not long after, the girl left her parents' home and moved to Seattle. Though their contact was now infrequent, Myra knew that Janet had not spoken to her father in the year since she had moved out.

But if her relationship with Janet explained Karp's hostility toward her, she knew that her own dislike of him had begun much earlier. Karp had antagonized Myra even before she was hired, when he and Rappaport had come to New York to interview her. "A rabbi," Karp had smirked. "What kind of job is that for a nice Jewish girl?" He had chuckled patronizingly, and Myra now recalled with shame that she had joined in. From then on, things went downhill. Within days of coming to the temple, Myra had seen through its power structure: she answered to Reuben Rappaport, and they both answered to Milton Karp.

It was her job as editor of the synagogue bulletin that prompted their first open conflict. Unhappy with several pieces Myra had published, Karp had himself appointed as the board's liaison to the bulletin. This meant he read and censored the journal before it went to press. He immediately used his position to cancel a column written by Myra that advocated feminist support groups in the sisterhood, calling it "inappropriate" for a synagogue newsletter.

Little escaped his attention. "I understand you missed teaching the confirmation class twice last month, Rabbi. Were you away on pressing synagogue business?"

"No, Milton," she replied, for it was his way to always call her Rabbi, and yet insist that she call him Milton. "I brought in other people to lecture on those days. They were experts in their areas."

"Of course, of course. Nonetheless, Rabbi, I think it would make a nice impression on our students if you seemed to be interested in the lectures you required them to attend."

Then came the inevitable Karp smile, followed by the thrust. "So that we have no mix-ups in the future, just tell me when you need to miss your classes. Okay?"

When she began counseling Janet, the tension accelerated. True to character, Karp never brought up the subject. But from what Janet told her, Myra knew that he was furious. Each time they met, Myra anticipated an explosion. But none came. Today, she had come to a deeper understanding of Milton Karp. It was not his way to attack directly. He provoked others to do it. That was why, even though he had orchestrated today's meeting, he had spoken only once, and at the end.

Minute by minute, Myra alternated between anger and depression. The difference between the two, she now knew, was slight. Depression was anger directed against yourself, anger was what you directed against others. When she thought of Karp she was enraged. But when she thought of the rest of the executive committee, she only felt dispirited. Despite her bravado at the meeting, she couldn't win in a congregational fight. And both she and Karp knew it.

She snatched up the book and flung it against the wall. Unfair. Unfair. She had sacrificed so much to become a rabbi. Everything. Even Evelyn. Evvie. Her greatest sacrifice. The Isaac she had been asked to slaughter to win acceptance by her God. She and Evvie had become friends two and a half years before she had finished rabbinical school in New York. They had met at the Women's Fitness Center. Soon they started running together. Two months later they became roommates. It was strange. She was becoming a rabbi and her roommate was not even a Jew. It took another four months before they admitted that their feelings for each other went deeper than just friendship. And another month of three A.M. discussions until they acted on those feelings. And then a glorious two years. Until Myra was almost ordained and offered this job. She knew her congregation would not understand why their female rabbi had moved out West with her non-Jewish female roommate. Or rather, they would understand. Too well.

Desperately, she resisted giving up Evvie. For three weeks she fantasized how she could live with her and still be a rabbi. But in moments of clarity she knew it would never work. Few professionals can be as easily destroyed by gossip and innuendo as rabbis. Also, although she loved Evvie, she didn't see herself as a lesbian. Evvie was simply a woman she had loved. Myra knew she wanted more than this relationship could offer. She wanted to love and be loved by a man. She wanted children. And she wanted to be a rabbi. Only later did she realize that Evvie had never really had a chance.

Two years later, it still hurt. There was still no man in her life. And now they wanted to fire her and stop her from being a rabbi.

For the hundredth time she picked up the envelope that had arrived two weeks earlier, on January 21—her birthday. Her address had been typed and there was no return address, but when Myra withdrew the single enclosed sheet there was no mistaking the handwriting. "No one will ever love you as much as I loved you. No one will ever hate you as much as I still hate you. I have not forgotten and I will not forgive."

She hadn't reread the note since the first time. But day after day, she found herself picking up the envelope, holding it, and wondering how she had provoked such hatred from a person who had once been so precious to her. She fingered the letter again. She felt very tired.

Ruth Karp was perplexed. Milton's behavior made no sense. She had expected him to come back from the temple exuberant. Instead, he sat in his armchair nursing his second glass of scotch and had greeted her attempts at communication with a mumbled, "Leave me alone." She could no longer restrain her curiosity.

"What happened when you saw Janet?"

"What the hell are you talking about?"

"You didn't see Janet?" she asked meekly.

"Janet's in Seattle. What the devil are you talking about?"

"Janet came here this morning. She flew in last night—she's moving back to LA. Milton, you wouldn't believe it. She looked so pretty, so relaxed. And she told me the most wonderful thing, that she wanted to see you, right away."

For the first time since coming home, the harsh lines of his face eased.

"So what happened?"

"I told her you were at the executive committee meeting, that it should be finishing about noon. She said she'd go to the temple and surprise you there at the end of the meeting."

"Well, she didn't show up," Milton said evenly, but his body went rigid.

Myra Wahl woke up from her short rest, angry again. Maybe that's good, she thought. At least it's better than depression. She sat up and looked at her watch: 7:45. An hour and a quarter to the show. She picked up *The Religious Manifesto* and found the passage she planned to attack. Distractedly, she inserted Evvie's envelope as a bookmark.

This meeting should have ended ten minutes ago, Daniel thought miserably. But Daryl Kelman would not let go. He leaned his lanky body over the rabbi's desk and scowled at him.

"It's *my* wedding, Rabbi. Can't you make any compromises?"

"On customs, maybe. On laws, no."

"Which means?"

"Which means that if you don't want Marcia to walk around you seven times under the huppah—the canopy, that is—she doesn't have to. But it also means that you're required to put the ring on her finger and say in Hebrew 'you are hereby sanctified unto me with this ring according to the laws of Moses and Israel.'"

"I told you already, I'll only do that if Marcia does the exact same thing."

Marcia Diskin broke in, her voice distraught. She pulled nervously at her short, dark hair.

"Daryl, I don't care."

"But I do. And it's not just me. Do you know how many faculty members will be there from the college? All I need is for them to see me acquiring you like I'm buying a slave. Don't you understand, Marcia, how terrible it will look? You don't say a single word during the entire service while I recite this formula. Like I'm buying a slave," he repeated roughly.

Marcia looked at Daniel, pleading.

"Oh, Rabbi, would it be so awful if I put the ring on Daryl's finger and said those words?"

"No. It wouldn't be awful at all. It just wouldn't be a religious Jewish wedding."

"Bullshit," exploded Daryl Kelman, and banged his fist on the desk. "It would be our wedding, done according to our religious convictions and as valid as anyone else's."

"If you're talking about validity in the eyes of California, you're right. But not in the eyes of Judaism. You see, Mr. Kelman, we're not just a religion, we're also a people. And when you're a member of a people you can't just arbitrarily disregard your people's way of doing things. For example, if a Jew keeps all the laws of the Sabbath on a Tuesday he might well have a personally fulfilling religious experience. But it wouldn't be a Jewish experience because his people don't keep the Sabbath on Tuesday. There are many beautiful things you can do at the wedding service that will make it a deep experience for both of you. But my job is to make sure that it's a Jewish wedding."

"Which means that Marcia stands there like a medieval dummy the whole time?"

Daniel looked at his watch in desperation. He had three minutes to solve this.

"When I got married, my wife and I were also bothered by the bride's passivity during the ceremony. We just found a less controversial solution. After I gave Rebecca the ring, she put a ring on my finger and said a verse from the Song of Songs, 'I am my beloved's and my beloved is mine.' I checked it with my grandfather, who was a rabbinic scholar. He was a little taken aback, but he looked into it and concluded that as long as the woman does not repeat the man's legally phrased formulation, there's no problem."

"Legal fictions!" Daryl sneered, tugging at his tie as if the air in the room was suffocating him.

"Please don't spoil things, Daryl," Marcia pleaded softly. She placed her hand on his arm.

It was not quite the ending Daniel had hoped for, but it would have to do. He stood up.

"I'm sorry, but I really must leave now."

The couple followed him out of the office, and then Marcia motioned to Daryl to wait, while she walked with Daniel to his car.

"I apologize for Daryl, Rabbi."

"There's no need to. But I was thinking, maybe I'm not the right rabbi for your wedding."

"Oh no, Rabbi. You have no idea how much I admire you. Why, I listen to you on the radio twice every week."

"But I'm only on once a week."

"What I mean is I always tape your show and listen a second time."

Daniel looked at her in wonderment. "*I* don't even have the tapes of my shows."

Marcia smiled shyly. A dimple appeared at the side of her cheek. "I guess that means I think you're the right rabbi for my wedding."

Myra Wahl paced relentlessly. She cursed Milton Karp, slammed her hand on the kitchen table, and began to scream aloud with pain and frustration—and then realized she had to calm down. And soon. There was just over an hour to the show. She pushed open her front door and stepped outside. It was surprisingly warm for a February evening in LA. She made a quick decision. Swiftly, she changed into her jogging suit and put on her Nikes. She tied on a light backpack and stuffed in Daniel's book. She would run to the studio; it was only about six miles. "No sweat," she said aloud, and laughed. What about coming home late at night? she thought. Ah, what the hell? I could use a runner's high.

She opened the door, breathed in several gulps of the clear night air, and locked the door behind her.

Sunday Night

Brenda and Daniel entered the KLAX studio at eight-forty. Daniel smiled a greeting at the burly, uniformed black man behind the desk, whose badge identified him as Henry Jefferson, Security.

"Mr. Winter, could you please have your guest sign in? It's a new security measure. We've been getting a lot of kooks lately."

"Are the panelists here yet?" Daniel asked, as Brenda entered her name in the log.

"All except the rabbi." At that moment, Jefferson's eyes swept toward the lit-up parking lot outside. "What the hell is that?"

Before Daniel and Brenda could turn around, a female jogger in her late twenties pushed open the door. She wore a bright green jogging suit with a white stripe down the sides, and her long, fine hair was swept back in a ponytail.

"Hello, Rabbi Wahl," said Daniel, emphasizing the title to warn the security guard.

"I'm a runner," Myra panted. "It focuses my thinking." She pushed in a button on her watch and read the figure. "Not bad. Forty-three minutes twelve seconds, and I've been here fifteen seconds already."

"But how you gonna get home, Rabbi?" asked Jefferson.

"Same way I came."

"There are a lot of nuts out there. You better watch your step."

Myra wavered between annoyance and civility. Henry Jefferson's race inclined her to the latter.

26

"I can take care of myself. Thank you."

Daniel introduced the two women as they started down the first of the two long corridors toward the studio.

"Still planning to destroy me, Myra?"

"I'm going to crucify you."

"That's dangerous talk for a Jew," Daniel laughed.

Before Myra could retort, Daniel felt a hand thump heavily on his shoulder. He turned to see Bartley Turner beaming at him. Turner, the director of programming for KLAX, was a chunky, middle-aged man who wore a perpetual grin. He drew heavily on his cigar, and the sickly smelling smoke wafted through the corridor.

"Need to see you for a minute, Dan."

Daniel gave Brenda and Myra directions to the office and told them to go ahead. Turner put an arm around him.

"What's up, Bartley?"

"Your ratings, for one thing. You now have the highest Sunday night ratings in LA." Bartley flourished the cigar triumphantly. "We think you have the potential to do more than *Religion and You*. Tuesday afternoon, Dick Stevens has to fly to Chicago. We want you to do an hour of his show."

"What guests have you lined up?"

"None, Danny boy. We know you can moderate and interview. We want to know if you can carry the ball for an hour all by your lonesome. A lot's going to be riding on how the show goes Tuesday. Think you can do it?"

"You bet I can!"

As he strode down the long hall, Daniel made no effort to restrain his imagination. His own show. No guests. Eventually something full-time. Maybe even national. The chance to spread a message, his message, to a congregation of five hundred thousand instead of a thousand. And what a congregation! Without a president asking where he'd been when he was out of his office or why he'd missed a morning service. The overhead clock jarred him out of his reverie. Ten minutes to show time.

He entered the office adjoining the studio. Myra Wahl and Joanne Short were immersed in animated conference by the far window—they were close friends, he knew—while Sister

Mary Kuluski and Brenda Goldstein were attempting polite conversation on the battered couch. As he walked by, he heard the nun telling Brenda about a conference she'd be flying to in New York that night, right after the show.

"Ladies," Daniel interrupted and saw Myra glare murderously at him.

"Clergy," he started over. "You all know the format of the show. You folks open it up, and then we take calls on your opening statements. Since the subject tonight is Feminism, Women, and Religion, I think it would be a good idea if you each speak two or three minutes on whatever you think is the most important issue facing women today."

The three nodded.

"One more thing. As you know, during the second hour of the show people call up with problems for which they want advice, religious or otherwise. Lately, most of the calls have gotten pretty boring. Which accounts for tonight's experiment. We've installed a device called a vocal metamorphizer. Its nickname is the 'scrambler,' and it makes callers' voices audible but unidentifiable. That way people won't feel self-conscious. The station has been advertising the scrambler the whole week, and I hope we're going to be getting much more interesting and personal calls tonight."

They headed for the studio. Six seats were set round a circular oak table with a microphone in front of each. Daniel invited Brenda inside, asking her to turn her microphone aside. The panelists tested their voices, and then Daniel explained the function of the cough button, to be pressed when a panelist felt a cough or sneeze coming.

At two minutes to nine, Reverend Joanne Short turned abruptly and looked Daniel straight in the eye.

"I've listened to this show many times. When you talk about religious issues, you treat them with one hundred percent respect. I will not tolerate one percent less in your treatment of feminism."

Daniel felt his stomach turn queasy.

Milton Karp steered erratically with his left hand while he spun the car radio dial with his right. Outside, the night was unusually clear for Los Angeles, but he was in no mood to notice. Ruth stopped his hand at a familiar voice: "This is Daniel Winter—Welcome to *Religion and You.*" Karp half listened, half daydreamed, as he heard Daniel move through the introductions. But his attention was suddenly caught at the mention of Myra Wahl, "the assistant rabbi of the Pico Boulevard Temple." Not for long, he thought savagely. "Rabbi Wahl is also a believer in a sound mind and a sound body. She is sitting here in a green jogging suit, and tells us that she will be jogging home after the show."

Ruth groaned. "She has no dignity. What are non-Jews going to think when they hear that? . . . Promise me one thing, honey. No more women rabbis."

She looked to her husband for a reaction. There was none. As if driving on automatic pilot, he turned onto Esther Avenue, their home block. Milton Karp's mind was far away.

Joanne Short spoke first. "The enemies of women are on the march, trying to take away from women the right to control their own bodies, which includes the free choice to terminate unwanted pregnancies. These people will not be satisfied until abortions are outlawed and the clothes-hanger abortionists are back in business. Opponents of abortion claim . . ."

This was the first time Daniel had met Joanne Short, though he had heard much about her and had invited her at Myra Wahl's insistence that for once the show have two real feminists, instead of a token representative. Looking at her, with her short straggly hair and faded blue jeans and sweater, he wondered how she was regarded at the University of the Southlands—this shrill voice of the sixties, whose opponents were always enemies. How did she relate to the button-down-shirted and long-skirted students of the 1980s, who cared more about their careers than about ushering in Woodstock? Maybe it was an error to have Myra Wahl and Joanne Short on together; maybe I'm not doing feminists any favor, he thought. He could hear Joanne Short's voice warming up for its final declaration. "We must never let the Moral Majority and the Catholic Church take this sacred right of free choice away from us. We will do whatever is necessary to stop them."

"Thank you, Reverend Short," Daniel said. "We will now hear from Sister Mary Kuluski." After Joanne Short's call to arms he found himself looking forward to two minutes of a more relaxed presentation.

"I'm a Catholic and a nun," the sister began softly, then straightened and spoke with resolution. "So you won't be surprised to learn that I disagree with Reverend Short. But I'm not going to debate with her now, because I want to speak with you on what I regard as the most important issue facing women . . . and men and children today. Peace. Not because I believe other issues confronting women aren't unimportant. They are. But if we don't solve the nuclear issue, there will be no one left to deal with the other issues. That is why saying we won't disarm until the Russians disarm is an *anti-religious* response to the issues of war and peace. The religious person does not wait for the nonreligious person to turn to God before he himself does so. Rather, he turns to God, confident that his example will influence his non-religious neighbors. Those who truly believe in God, in God's grace, must advocate nuclear disarmament immediately, confident that their example will influence the hearts of our brothers and sisters, even in the Soviet Union."

She stopped, and the words just spun out of Daniel's mouth, though he knew he should be quiet until the opening statements were finished.

"And if our example does not influence the Soviet Union, but they take advantage of our disarmament to overpower or destroy us?"

"Well, Daniel," the nun replied, unruffled, "my religion teaches that it's better to be among the victims than the murderers. Certainly, our Saviour could easily have destroyed the Roman soldiers who came to crucify him. He preferred to die, rather than shed the blood of his murderers. I know of no better example to follow than that."

"So you're saying all wars are wrong?"

"Yes."

"Including World War Two?"

"Yes."

"And were the Jews wrong for revolting in the Warsaw ghetto?"

"Of course I'm not condemning them. What they did was human and very understandable. But we are called upon to be more than human, to be God-like, to stop the cycle of violence."

"One last question, Sister. Adolf Hitler caused the deaths of about fifty-five million people. It seems to *me* that the most religious act anyone could have done between 1939 and 1945 would have been to kill him and thus prevent massive human suffering. I'm curious. If you knew someone who during World War Two had the opportunity to kill Hitler, but refrained from doing so for religious reasons, how would you regard that person?"

"As a moral hero," the nun answered. She was clearly uncomfortable at the animosity she saw on Myra Wahl's face and at the grim look on Daniel's face. "And how would you regard such a person, Daniel?" she asked him.

"As an accessory to all of Hitler's later murders."

Daniel saw Brenda Goldstein looking at him with a smile in her eyes, and he felt like walking over and hugging her. It seemed to him at that moment that he would welcome anything Myra Wahl might say.

He was wrong.

"I'm speaking now as a rabbi," she began, "so I'm addressing these comments to Jews. I'm not going to speak about a current challenge to women, but rather about a recent failure of both Jewish women and men." She paused. "I was extremely disappointed with the indifference of most of the Jewish community to the passage of the Equal Rights Amendment. Well, the ERA is now dead, but I still have a question I want to ask you. How could you have been so immoral, and maybe even worse—so foolish? Didn't you realize that the people opposing the ERA are the same kind of people who burned Jews during World War Two? And now that it's no longer fashionable to gas Jews or lynch blacks, women have become the new kikes and niggers. . . ."

Daniel fingers squeezed down on the censor button. There was a four-second delay before her words would go on the air. The delay was a safety measure to prevent callers from using any of the seven words forbidden to be broadcast. Never before had Daniel pushed the button to censor a clergyman's language. For that matter, "kike" and "nigger" were not among the seven words. But, dammit, this show is volatile enough, he thought furiously. I don't need to get Jewish Defense League and Black Panther types taking off after me.

As Myra launched into her conclusion, oblivious of Daniel's action, he glanced over his left shoulder into the small room where Jim Bell sat. The dark-skinned, perpetually scowling young man answered all the phone calls, deciding which had possibilities and, most importantly, screening out the oddballs. Several of them had already called tonight. The first rang in at 9:01, just after the introductions.

"I want to tell the so-called Reverend Short that God did not intend for women to be ordained. She is an ally of Satan . . ."

"Thank you," Bell said firmly and slammed down the receiver. The next kook checked in at 9:03 with a request that the rabbi confirm or deny the authenticity of "the Protocols of the Elders of Zion which Henry Ford printed and which the Jews have suppressed." As for the other calls, it took the skilled Bell about fifteen seconds each to determine if they were of general interest or not. The promising ones—Paul–abortion, Robin–ERA, Sean–disarmament—he punched up on the screen in front of Daniel. At 9:10, as Myra Wahl was concluding, Daniel caught Bell's eye. The young man raised his hands in exasperation—the calls were coming in heavy.

Daniel pushed a button.

"Paul, you're on the air. Who would you like to speak to?"

"Reverend Short. . . . Reverend, do you believe people have a right to commit suicide?"

The three panelists looked a little bewildered at the question, and Daniel flashed Jim Bell a puzzled glance.

"Generally, no," Joanne Short replied. "But why are you asking?"

"Because you say that the right to abortion naturally

follows from a woman's right to do what she wants with her body. But if men and women have the right to do what they want with their bodies, then don't they have the right to commit suicide?"

Joanne Short sensed Daniel's unsuppressed grin and shot him an angry glance.

"Paul, I think your analogy is farfetched. People who commit suicide are usually acting under great mental stress. It's questionable that they are even acting out of free will. So of course we want to restrain them. But abortion is the free-will expression of a woman who wants to terminate an unwanted—"

"Terminate?" the caller cut in harshly. "Isn't that just a fancy word for murder?"

"That's sick," Joanne Short snapped. "A fetus is a fetus, not a human being."

"But isn't the real reason you feminists popularized the word fetus so that people could avoid confronting what they were doing? My sister gave birth a few months ago, and the whole time she was pregnant she never called it a fetus, only a baby. It's only the person who wants to get rid of their child who calls it a fetus."

Sister Mary Kuluski signaled to speak.

"I agree with you, Paul. We Catholics are pro-life because we believe that human life is sacred from the second it's conceived. Nothing could ever justify destroying such a life."

"What if the pregnancy were the result of rape or incest?" asked Daniel.

"If we wouldn't kill a child who resulted from rape or incest *after* it was born, what right do we have to kill it before? Life is life from the moment of conception." The sister was silent for a moment and then turned to Myra, "What's the Jewish view of when life begins?"

Daniel interjected, "Jews believe a fetus is a fetus until it graduates from medical school."

Everyone laughed except Myra. Paul was forgotten.

"According to Exodus, a murderer is put to death. But one who destroys a *fetus*," Myra spoke icily, "pays a fine. Because our Bible doesn't believe that a fetus is a human being. That's why we Reform Jews believe in free choice for women. And I must tell you, Sister, that I view attempts by your church and certain other religious groups to impose their parochial views of abortion on all Americans as a violation of the First Amendment." Sister Mary's thin shoulders stiffened. "Women are no longer chattel. They have the right to be mothers if they want, and they also have the right to choose not to be mothers. As you have chosen, Sister."

Daniel looked over at Sister Mary, now responding in what seemed like unusual vehemence for so pacific a personality. Of course a fetus was not the same as a human being, he said to himself. After all, had Catholics ever designated a miscarriage as a death to be commemorated with prayers and rituals? And yet Mary Kuluski would impose on a raped woman nine months of carrying inside her body the child of the man she probably hated most in the world. He himself infinitely preferred the approach of a nineteenth-century Hasidic rabbi who ruled that a raped woman could have an abortion because "daughters of Israel are not soil that must nourish a seed planted in them against their will." On the other hand, the Joanne Shorts and Myra Wahls who made abortion sound as morally unproblematic as removing an aching tooth were hardly attractive alternatives. He knew from his own counseling experience that there were some women who, in effect, used abortion as the ultimate method of birth control. Abortion rights without a sense of responsibility, even guilt, just seemed too dangerous. Once life and death were taken out of God's hands, where would it end? Suddenly, he became conscious of the silence in the studio and yanked himself out of his reverie. He pushed in a button while reading the monitor—"Hello, Sean, you're on the air."

The grandfather clock gave off its hourly chime. Ten o'clock. Milton Karp stood up from his chair and stretched.

"I'm restless, honey. I'm going out again."

"At this hour?"

"I want to take a drive, relax a bit, and think. Okay?"

Ruth put down the sweater she was knitting and stared up at him. He did not meet her eyes.

"What's the matter, Milt?"

"Nothing." He laughed mirthlessly. "Nothing's the matter."

"You're worrying me. If it weren't serious you wouldn't be acting like this. You know you're going to tell me about it sooner or later—so why not make it sooner?" She came over and stood beside him.

"You know what's the matter?" he exploded, vehement in his anger. "Your big-mouth daughter told Myra about . . ." Pain and fear stopped him abruptly.

"About what?"

"About what happened in Chicago."

"What's Wahl planning, Milt?"

"To blackmail me."

"Oh, no—"

"If I force her to resign, she's threatened to spread the news to everyone."

"Maybe you should back down then, Milt. Just wait for her contract to expire."

"It's too late. The whole executive committee wants her out. At this point even *I* can't stop them. Now do you understand why I've been going crazy the whole day, why I need some time alone?"

"Oh, Milton, I'm worried."

He pulled on his jacket. "Well, don't be. I'll take care of Myra Wahl. And everything's gonna be all right."

10:06. Brenda flashed Daniel a thumbs-up sign. He smiled. The show was clearly going well. It wasn't just that there was controversy, but it was *good* controversy. About important issues—abortion, pacifism, feminism. Listeners would learn that if they wanted high-level discussions on the most important ethical issues they'd have to consider religious approaches. What other societal institutions were even trying to give people a sense of moral direction? Universities? The mass media? Psychoanalysts' couches?

The scrambler was working out well. People were calling in and really opening up. He felt good about the show. And about himself. And, he thought as he looked over to his left, about Brenda.

Daniel glanced at the monitor. The top name was Ian—abortion. It was almost an hour since the last call on the subject. He pushed in the button.

"Hello, Ian. Who would you like to speak to?"

"Wahl and Short," a low voice replied.

"That would be *Rabbi* Wahl and *Reverend* Short," Daniel interjected. "Now, what is your question?"

"Since the court legalized abortion in 1973, over ten million babies have been murdered in America. That's bigger than the Holocaust the Rabbi referred to before . . ."

Bell usually screens out the nuts, Daniel thought, but this one got through. I'd better cut the damage.

"Ian," he broke in, "we went through this subject at some length before. So if you have a question, please get to it."

"Just a thought for *Ms.* Reverend and *Ms.* Rabbi. You give women the right to murder babies. Maybe someone's gonna give us the right to kill *you*."

The line went dead.

"On behalf of *Religion and You*," Daniel broke in quickly, noting the burning anger on the faces of the two feminists, "I wish to apologize to Rabbi Wahl and Reverend Short for that abusive call. Now, I don't want to waste any more time discussing it." He pushed in a button.

"You're on the air, Laura. To whom would you like to speak?"

The only response was quick, intense breathing.

"Take your time. It's all right."

Silence.

Daniel looked over at Jim Bell, who drew his hand across his throat. He was about to follow Bell's advice to hang up, when the caller spoke.

"That's not my name."

"What?"

"My name's not Laura. . . . Is my identity really protected?"

"This machine alters your voice patterns," Daniel explained gently, alert to the quiver in the woman's voice. "I'm told that even people who know you well won't recognize your voice."

Silence again. And then a sound which Daniel guessed to be a stifled sob.

Myra leaned toward the microphone.

"This is Rabbi Wahl. I think I can understand what you're feeling. God knows I've felt the same way often enough."

"I don't know where to begin."

"Begin at the end," Myra said, in an unusually gentle tone.

"My husband just got out of prison. He was in for a year and a half."

The panelists looked at each other, ill at ease.

"Is he having trouble finding work?" Daniel asked, to fill the silence.

"You don't understand. My husband never should have been released."

"Excuse me, Laura." It was Joanne Short. "If he was only in prison for a year and a half it doesn't sound like he was in for anything very serious."

"They put him away for something else. They don't know what he's really done." The woman hesitated, but when she spoke again the words spilled out. "I found something. . . . I got him angry yesterday. He hit me. I'm frightened. . . ."

Laura's soft voice broke off. They waited. The seconds ticked away. Nothing.

"Listen, Laura," said Joanne Short, flashing a concerned look at Myra, "we're here to help you. If this man is threatening you . . ."

For the first time in Daniel's two years on the show the door marked "Do not open while show is in progress" was gently eased open. Daniel looked up in surprise as the director of programming, Bartley Turner, came over to him.

"Get her off quickly," Turner hissed through his teeth. "She might be looney tunes, and she could be libelous."

Immediately, Daniel cut in on Joanne Short's attempts at reassurance.

"Laura, I want you to know that we all want to help you, but it sounds like some of what we're talking about might better be discussed in private. We're going to break now for a few minutes of public service announcements. But don't hang up, and we'll keep talking."

Daniel was motioning for engineer Bob Watson to activate the prerecorded announcements, when Myra Wahl spoke. "We're not deserting you, Laura. Stay on, and I'm going to arrange to get together with you first thing tomorrow morning."

Daniel pressed the cough button, shutting off his microphone.

"Finished?" he asked Myra.

She nodded.

The public service messages came on. Myra jumped up. "I'll handle it," she said, and ran into Jim Bell's room, where she picked up the phone. When the engineer flashed Daniel a warning that the messages were finishing, he tapped on the little window that was his lookout into Bell's office. Myra acknowledged him and quickly returned to her seat.

Forty-five minutes later the show erupted again.

"As we get into the last few minutes of what has been a very special evening," Daniel said, "let me ask our visiting clergy if they have any final thoughts on what most bothers American women today?"

"You know what's bothering American women?" Myra Wahl turned to him sharply. "I'll tell you, Daniel. It's the sort of sexist nonsense that you yourself perpetuated in *The Religious Manifesto.*"

Daniel drew in a deep breath, felt his chest tighten, and exhaled very slowly. Myra flipped open his book to the marked page. "A quote from page 106," she began. "'It is the genius of Orthodox Judaism that it has designated specific rituals that are solely the province of males.' And with this, you proclaim as *genius* a way of life that excludes women from the rabbinate, that vests the right of divorce solely in the hands of the husband, and that has its males make a blessing every morning thanking God they're not women. Though, given the way they treat women, I suppose that blessing makes sense."

"I think you're being demagogic, Rabbi Wahl." Daniel's voice sounded formal and distant, even to his own ears. "First of all, I wasn't writing about the things you just mentioned, and in any case your presentation of them was simplistic and unfair. The point that I was making in my book was that religions that assign precisely the same rituals to men and women soon discover that men become less involved in the religion than women. The popular stereotype of Catholicism, which I think has some justification, is that women are more apt to drag their husbands to mass than the reverse." To his relief, Daniel saw Mary Kuluski smiling at his comment. He continued. "When I visited the Far East I found a similar pattern. The men might be the monks but it was the women who filled the temples. And the same is true of most Jews. While men might still be the leaders of Reform and Conservative Judaism, women are much more involved in the synagogue's religious life than men. In the Jewish world, it's only among the Orthodox, where men have responsibilities that only they can fulfill, that men remain as involved in religion as women. That's what I meant when I spoke of the genius of Orthodoxy."

"So what does that say about men?" Myra jeered, the color rising in her cheeks. "That the moment women have equality they stop playing the game?"

"If you're saying that it reveals ugly things about men, you may be right. Maybe men have to feel a special dominance outside of the home to make up for women's specialness inside it. Maybe," and he half-smiled, "it's because men have more testosterone."

"Which means?"

"That men are more aggressive than women and their aggression has to be channeled into healthy outlets. And that maybe they need their own areas of domain. And that perhaps if women do the same things men do they'll just drive men into less healthy activities."

"So women should limit their aspirations because of the testosterone difference?" There was no mistaking the rising contempt in Myra's voice.

Bob Watson signaled frantically that there were only fifteen seconds left.

"I'm not saying that. But I do wish you'd have the

openness to recognize that the social policies you're advocating will have massive ramifications, and some of them—"

"And I wish," Myra shouted, "you had the honesty to recognize that you're using science the way Hitler used science."

Whether her timing was intentional or not, Daniel would never know. But he did know that with Myra's furious words, they had run out of time. "This is Daniel Winter, saying goodnight for *Religion and You*," was all he had time to say.

Inside the studio there was dead silence.

Myra was the first to break the silence, her eyes for once downcast. "I'm sorry, Daniel."

"I'm sure."

"I wasn't calling you a Nazi. What I meant was . . ."

"You were very successful in communicating what you wanted to communicate, that I was like Hitler."

"I'm sorry," she repeated, dull patches of red on her cheeks. "You really got me angry. But I went too far, and I apologize."

"Thank you very much. You insult me in front of a quarter of a million people and apologize to me in private. Well, good for you. Only don't expect me to accept your apology."

He went over to the door, grabbing his jacket.

"I really am sorry."

"Why don't you try me again before Yom Kippur?" he snapped and walked out of the room.

By the time Brenda caught up with him, he was almost out of the building. She put a hand on his arm.

"Calm down, Daniel. The show was terrific."

Daniel walked on, his blue eyes staring fixedly ahead. "I can't stand that woman," he said through his teeth.

"What she did was disgusting. But you know, I think she's truly sorry."

"That, as they say in New York, and a dollar will get you on the subway."

"Come on. We'll get a bite to eat and you'll feel better."

He shook his head.

"I'm sorry, Brenda. She really upset me. I have to be alone."

He saw the disappointment reflected in her eyes.

"Please let me have a raincheck on our dinner. . . . I'm sorry. . . . I'm too upset to be decent company tonight."

Sister Mary Kuluski passed by and heard him. "Don't be upset. It was a good program. And since you're a rabbi, Daniel, I feel I can say this to you. You'd like yourself a lot better if you forgave her."

Daniel said nothing. He carefully avoided catching the eye of Myra Wahl as she came past them. Myra shrugged helplessly at Brenda and then stepped outside, activated her stopwatch, and ran off into the darkness surrounding the parking lot.

"Do you really hate her that much?" Brenda asked.

"Tonight I do," said Daniel, running his hands through his hair. "That's why I have to be alone. If I don't talk now, Brenda, I won't say anything foolish. . . . Good night."

Abruptly, he left her and went out to his car. Brenda stared after him and then went back to the studio to pick up her jacket. She passed Joanne Short in the hallway.

"Poor Myra," Joanne Short said to her. "She's been under a terrible strain recently. She really felt bad about what she said." She looked at Brenda, waiting for a response. There was none. "It was wrong of Daniel not to accept her apology."

"My grandmother was murdered at Auschwitz, Reverend Short. And if somebody compared me to Hitler it would take me a long time to forgive them."

Brenda went into the studio and retrieved her jacket. What a night! she thought. She looked around, and saw *The Religious Manifesto* lying on the table. Myra must have forgotten it. She picked up the book and walked out.

Sunday Midnight

Myra Wahl turned off from the bustling traffic of Pico Boulevard to the greater calm of Gateway. She hugged close to the sidewalk, and the few oncoming cars passed wide of her. She was feeling calmer now. Running always did that to her. But more importantly, she had come to a decision. She was not going to expose Milton Karp. God knows, he deserved it. But she had not come all this way, become a rabbi, just to be a blackmailer. She would leave the temple. She could accept that now. Why stay in a place where the people were too angry to let you influence them? If she made an agreement with Karp the whole thing could be done without unpleasantness. She'd move to a new pulpit and be there by the time the High Holidays came. A good time for starting over.

At this moment she didn't even regret her attack on Daniel Winter. She had held in so much rage for so long that it had to erupt. Now that the explosion had passed she felt calmer. She'd call Winter in the morning. And she'd apologize again, and again, and sooner or later he'd have to accept it. She'd even go on the show and make a formal apology if he demanded it, though God knows, she wouldn't retract one word of her other criticisms.

And she knew that the time had come to seek out Evvie. Not to get back together. Despite all the loneliness of these last two years, getting back together with Evvie was not what she wanted for herself. But she had hurt this woman far more than she had ever before realized. Somehow she would find a way to make things okay.

The hum of an approaching automobile interrupted her

thoughts. She swung around and jogged backwards a few paces. In the distance all she could see were the approaching lights of a large car. She turned back and resumed her normal strides. A few seconds later she twisted around again. The noise of the engine sounded much closer than it should have. Pedaling backwards she moved toward the sidewalk. She gestured, trying to catch the driver's eye. But the brights were now on, blinding her. Instinctively she looked down. The wheels of the car were turning, turning—they were coming directly at her. She moved faster, half paralyzed with fear. But not fast enough. She screamed.

Her body sailed twenty feet before it landed.

Monday

The phone rang. Automatically, Daniel groped for the watch on his nightstand and checked the time: six-thirty A.M. "God Almighty," he groaned. He picked up the receiver and registered a groggy hello.

"It's Brenda. Did I wake you?"

"No. I was just getting up to answer the phone." He had wanted to say that to somebody for a long time, but he had always forgotten. Now there was no response.

"I have bad news, Daniel." His heart started pumping adrenaline, and he was immediately alert. "Myra Wahl's body was found early this morning."

"What!"

"Jogging home from the show she was hit by a car. She was going down a quiet stretch on Gateway. She didn't have a chance. He must have been doing sixty."

"A drunk driver?"

"We don't know."

"What does he say?"

"Who?"

"The driver?"

"Nothing. We don't have him, Daniel. It was hit-and-run."

Daniel sighed and rubbed his forehead.

"Brenda, my mind's still unfocused. I'm not absorbing this yet. I'm going to synagogue for morning services, and then I'll come to your office."

She gave him directions.

* * *

At around seven-thirty that morning the phone rang in the Karp home. Ruth picked it up and heard Rabbi Reuben Rappaport greet her. "Have you heard?" he began, and then hurried on, without waiting for a response. "The police just called me. It won't even be on the news until ten. It's tragic, simply tragic." Ruth's alarmed exclamation was turned away with a Yiddish proverb, "Man plans and God laughs." Finally, he told her that Myra Wahl was dead.

Her first reaction was an immense relief. I suppose I should be ashamed, she thought. But then again, why? Myra Wahl had alienated Janet from her father and had threatened to expose Milton for a crime for which he had long since paid. She would go to the funeral as social etiquette required. Even to the cemetery. And maintain a look of stricken solemnity on her face. But that was all. She would do no more.

She went upstairs to wake Milton. She had intended to let him sleep, but the information was too momentous to keep. When she told him, his reaction surprised her. "Dead?" he said, his voice a ragged whisper. Then silence. A few minutes later he barked out one question, "Why the hell hasn't Janet come home?" Ruth Karp went back downstairs. She started cleaning the kitchen. But the work couldn't distract her. Something was very wrong.

"Hello, Brenda."

Startled out of her deep concentration, Brenda Goldstein looked up from the notes on her desk. Daniel held out six long-stemmed red roses to her.

"For yesterday evening. You shouldn't suffer for my bad moods."

She raised the blossoms to her face and inhaled. A smile lit her green eyes.

Five minutes later they were seated in Senior's, a restaurant just behind homicide headquarters. Brenda ordered a cheese omelet with extra toast and lots of coffee, "I've been up since four," she explained. "I'm ravenous."

Daniel restricted himself to coffee. "There's not much that's kosher here, I suspect."

They managed to postpone the inevitable for a little

longer, speaking of Jessica, the synagogue, the unseasonably mild winter weather, and Brenda's ability, which Daniel coveted, to eat extra toast while staying slim. Finally, Brenda took the last bite of her omelet. Setting down her fork, she leaned back and let out a long breath.

"Okay. Let me tell you what we know as of now. That is, facts plus some speculation. . . . Fact: Myra Wahl was struck and killed by a car at 12:04 A.M.—"

"12:04?" Daniel stopped her. "The witnesses were that precise?"

"There were no witnesses. As a matter of fact, her body was not discovered until almost one A.M. The car that struck her was going so fast that the impact sent her flying. She landed next to a building, far enough from the road so that the people in passing cars wouldn't see her."

"And nobody heard anything?"

"Do you know that stretch of Gateway, near Bradley? It's a little enclave of small buildings in an industrial park. It only runs for three blocks before the neighborhood becomes residential again. But nobody lives on those blocks."

"So how was she discovered?"

"Two high school kids parked on Bradley to make out and found the body."

"Wait a second." Daniel frowned. "I don't understand how we know that she was killed at 12:04. Autopsies can't be so precise."

"We had a bit of luck on the time factor. Whether it was the impact of the collision or of the fall itself, Myra Wahl's watch was smashed. At 12:04 and thirty-one seconds, to be precise."

Daniel gnawed on his lower lip.

"What's troubling you?"

"12:04. It's an odd time. You and I saw Myra start running right after the show. That would have been no later than 11:05. She was a good runner. Remember, when she came in she told us that it had only taken her forty-something minutes to get to the studio. I presume she meant from her house. But she was killed last night a full hour after she started running, and she wasn't even halfway home. Strange, isn't it?"

"It is strange," Brenda agreed. "But not disturbing."

"What does that mean?"

"In every homicide investigation we come across inconsistencies. And they can almost always be made to sound ominous. But they rarely are. It's only because Myra Wahl is dead and can't explain to us what happened that they remain a mystery. In actuality, she could have done any number of things. For example, when she was leaving the show and you ignored her, she flashed me an upset look. Maybe she stopped off in a coffee shop and brooded for a little while."

"But we saw her running!"

"We saw her starting to run. Maybe she got tired, and walked part of the way. There are a million possibilities, Daniel. Maybe she ran into a friend?"

"At eleven-thirty P.M.?"

"Yes. At eleven-thirty P.M. Maybe somebody she knew drove by and stopped to speak with her." Daniel nodded reflectively. "Do you see what I mean? I've already come up with three plausible explanations."

"Okay. Okay. I'm not totally convinced, but I get your point. What else do you know?"

"Within a day or two we'll have a pretty good idea of the car that did it."

"How?"

"There's a trim ring around the headlight that popped off when she was struck. Also some shattered headlight glass, not a lot, was found at the scene. Headlight trims and headlight glass are distinctive. At the very least, forensics will be able to narrow it down to the make of the car and if we're lucky, maybe even the year. Also, there's a good chance there's going to be a brush trace."

"A what?"

"A brush trace," Brenda repeated patiently. Daniel would have been surprised to learn that Brenda's expertise on hit-and-run accidents had been acquired in the last four hours. "When a car hits clothing it leaves a mark, and those marks are as singular as fingerprints. Given the speed at which Myra Wahl was struck, the boys in the lab are pretty sure there will be some very distinct markings on her jogging outfit. Between the broken bits of the car and the brush trace, we catch a lot of hit-and-run drivers."

"You sound pretty involved in the case."

"Cerezzi—that's my boss, Lieutenant Joe Cerezzi—thinks it's time for me to get my feet wet. He says I'll be able to help the department a lot more if I learn how police actually solve crimes. So he's assigned me to work closely with him in investigating this case. An easier case, he said, than last night's other two homicides—a woman strangled in her apartment and another knifed in an alleyway. I'll tell you, though, I still can't get over the fact that in the first case I'm really involved with, the victim turns out to be someone I've met. You know, with her death coming right after that threatening phone call, I just feel so spooky."

"Me too," said Daniel. He sat quietly, rolling a section of his *Los Angeles Times* into a cylinder. Tighter and tighter. "I just wish it were last night again."

Brenda's puzzled eyes studied his dark expression.

"Since you called me this morning, I've been in agony. It's odd, isn't it? I never cared for Myra Wahl. Last night, I even hated her. Or at least I thought I did. But since this morning one thought has been obsessing me. Why didn't I forgive her?"

Absently, he put down the paper and ran his fingers up and down his temples.

"It's not your fault, Daniel. You had every right to be angry. The lady virtually called you a Nazi on radio."

"But she asked me to forgive her three times."

"I don't care if she asked you a dozen times. The incident had just happened. You were hurt."

"You don't understand." His voice hoarsened with intensity. "It's a basic Jewish law. If someone hurts you and sincerely asks forgiveness, you *must* grant it. If you're still upset, the law recognizes that you might refuse once, even twice. But after the third request you must forgive them. Myra asked me three times. The funny thing is I was aware of that last night. But I didn't want to forgive her. Now," he went on miserably, "I can't forgive myself."

"Daniel, last year at synagogue on Yom Kippur you spoke about the steps involved in repentance. Right?"

"You remember?"

"There *are* advantages in going to synagogue only three days a year," she smiled gently. "Things make a big impression. Anyway, if I recall what you said, when Myra Wahl asked your forgiveness, she was following one of the steps in repentance. Am I right?"

He nodded.

"What are the other steps?"

"There's an order. First, to recognize that you have sinned. Next, as much as possible, to undo the damage you've done. Then, to ask forgiveness, and of course, don't do it again."

"Well, maybe this sounds harsh, but it doesn't seem to me that you owed Myra Wahl forgiveness last night."

"Why not? The more I think about it, the more I realize that she really was sorry. And knowing Myra, I'm sure it wasn't easy for her to apologize."

"All true. But if there are steps in repentance, then she skipped one. She knew that she had done wrong and she asked your forgiveness. But she didn't undo the damage."

"What could she have done?"

"The irony is," Brenda said loudly, and then lowered her voice as the waiter passed by the table, "that you yourself told her last night. Remember what you snapped at her, that she insulted you in public and apologized in private. You had every right to expect a public apology. *Then*, you would have been obligated to forgive her."

Daniel forced a smile.

"Thank you, Brenda. What you're saying is true. I know that. But I still don't feel good about myself."

"Wait a minute. Let me ask you. That Jewish law about asking forgiveness three times, what does it mean—that you have to ask three times or on three different occassions?"

"What are you thinking?"

"Well, it seems to me that it must mean three different occasions. Otherwise, whenever a person asks for forgiveness and is refused they'd immediately ask twice more. But the hurt party needs time to get over their hurt. So the law must mean that the offender has to ask forgiveness on three occasions."

This time his smile was genuine.

"The day my movement starts ordaining women as rabbis I'm recommending you as a candidate."

Brenda looked at her watch.

"If I don't get back to the office soon, I might be needing that recommendation. Why don't you come up with me? I have something to give you."

The clutter on her desk had increased in the hour they were gone. There was now a bulging folder on hit-and-run accidents in Los Angeles County, six pink slips with calls to be returned, and a long handwritten note from Lieutenant Cerezzi taped to the milk bottle that held the roses. Daniel scanned the crowded bookshelf in the office while Brenda perused Cerezzi's note. Her eyebrows drew together.

"Anything wrong?"

She hesitated. "It's nothing." She dug under the mess and extracted a book. "Myra Wahl's copy of *The Religious Manifesto*. She left it at the studio last night, and I picked it up for her. Now I can't think of anyone—aside from you—who might want it."

"Thanks for the compliment," he dead-panned, taking the book.

Brenda flushed prettily and suppressed a smile. "You know that's not what I meant. By the way, the funeral is at the Pico Boulevard Temple tomorrow, eleven A.M. Are you going?"

"I, and probably most of the rabbis in LA."

"I'm going to be there, too."

"Is that standard police practice?"

"As a matter of fact, it is. Particularly in a case like this, where the killing was presumably accidental. The criminal might feel guilty and show up. We'll have a few police there, scattered around, seeing if anyone looks out of place."

She looked down bleakly at her crowded desk.

"Well," Daniel began, "I guess . . ."

She stopped him, her eyes still downward. "Daniel, I have to ask you something."

"So ask."

"Please don't be angry."

"Okay," he smiled at her. "I promise not to be angry."

"What did you do last night after the show?"

He stared at her, quiet, absorbing the question.

"Daniel, I'm asking because I have to. Rationally and, yes, emotionally, I know you're not involved. But last night you were furious at Myra. I wasn't the only one to witness that fury. So I have to ask. What did you do last night?"

"I drove around for a little while and then went home."

"When you left me, you were so upset that I was worried. I called your house to see if you were all right. But you didn't answer."

"That makes sense. As I said, I drove around a bit. I needed to calm down."

"Daniel, the last call I made was at almost one A.M.."

He reddened.

"I guess I stayed out later than I thought. What more can I tell you? It's not like there are a dozen witnesses who saw me. Look, Brenda, I know it isn't pleasant to ask me such questions. But what can I offer as proof? I can only assure you of what I hope you know is true, that I didn't leave the studio and run over Myra Wahl. Any other questions?"

"No," said Brenda.

"I'm going, then. I'll see you . . . well, certainly tomorrow, at the funeral."

He left.

She sat motionless, staring at the empty space where he had been standing. Then she reread Joe Cerezzi's note. "A Reverend Joanne Short came in this morning at 9:30. She told me that last night, about an hour before she was killed, Myra Wahl had an extremely rancorous argument with a Rabbi Daniel Winter. According to Reverend Short, Wahl repeatedly tried to make peace with the rabbi, but he refused. She gave me your name as a witness, said you were a guest of the rabbi. Prudence suggests that we contact him and find out his movements for last night. If you're uncomfortable doing this because you know him, I understand. But otherwise, precisely because you do know him, maybe you could handle it."

Brenda Goldstein remained at her desk, staring at the roses in front of her. *I just flubbed my first assignment,* she thought. But she knew that that wasn't what was really bothering her.

Monday Afternoon

The rest of that day Daniel devoted to his rabbinical duties: two hours visiting sick congregants, a lunch meeting with synagogue president Wilbur Kantor and education chairman Raymond Wexler, to discuss the declining enrollment in the Hebrew school ("The average age of Jews in this country is forty-six, and that's also hurting us," Daniel told them), and then back to his office, where he dictated to Pat Hastings six uninspired letters. He groaned when he saw it was not yet four o'clock.

Freed of all immediate obligations, Daniel sat at his desk brooding. He picked up Myra Wahl's copy of *The Religious Manifesto* and started rereading the chapter on men and women that had so offended her. It was on the fifth page that he came across the envelope that had been her bookmark.

He examined the small envelope. The postmark from New York was more than two weeks old. There was no return address. Impulsively, perhaps because he was bored rereading material he knew too well, he opened the envelope and read the letter. Later, he could find no justification for what he had done. Rationalizations, yes. Myra Wahl was dead; there was no real moral issue of invasion of privacy. And because she had been murdered, every detail had to be checked out.

But these pangs of conscience were to come later. Now, he read the short note that Myra Wahl had carried with her the day of her death: "No one will ever love you as much as I loved you. No one will ever hate you as much as I still hate you. I have not forgotten and I will not forgive." He did not know how long he sat there, the note between his fingers.

He reached for the phone and dialed Reuben Rappaport at the Pico Boulevard Temple. Rappaport gave him the information he sought, that Myra Wahl's parents would be staying at the Holiday Inn in Westwood. "I'm picking them up at the airport at 4:45, but if you could spend some time with them later, Daniel, it would be a merciful thing. I think talking to Myra's colleagues would be the greatest consolation they could have at this moment." One thing's for certain, Daniel thought, Reuben Rappaport had not been one of his listeners last night.

His second call was to the homicide division. He caught Brenda Goldstein on her way out. "Wait for me a half hour," he said excitedly. "I'm bringing you some information on this case that I think is dynamite."

He rushed out of his office. "Running to a fire?" Pat teased as he passed her deak.

He had no bantering retort. He inserted the note into the Xerox machine and made two copies. And then left without saying good-bye.

"I don't think Myra Wahl's death was accidental," Daniel told Brenda.

"Neither do we," she said in an even voice.

He was caught off guard by her reply.

"Lieutenant Cerezzi was in right after you called," Brenda went on. "We just got the report from the lab. They were out there examining the accident site, and they told Cerezzi that the angle at which Myra's body was struck indicates that the car's wheels were directed straight at her. Which means that unless the driver was swerving to avoid something else, an unlikely occurrence on Gateway at midnight—Myra Wahl was run down intentionally. Now what brings you here?"

"I think I know who the murderer is."

Brenda stared at him.

"I think Myra was murdered by the writer of this letter," Daniel said, handing her the envelope. He told Brenda where he had found it. She grabbed the phone, and two minutes later, Lieutenant Joe Cerezzi was in the room. A burly Italian cop in his late forties, Cerezzi had a slight paunch and dark, narrow, appraising eyes. He greeted Daniel with a crushing handshake and a broad smile. The last faded quickly as he read the note.

"Mmm. Interesting."

"That's the understatement of the year." Daniel shook his head. "Doesn't this make things pretty obvious?"

"Maybe, maybe not."

The lieutenant's smooth manner was unnerving Daniel.

"Explain something to me, Lieutenant," he said impatiently. "A woman is killed in circumstances that increasingly indicate premeditation. We find a letter only two weeks old, from someone with a declared vendetta against her. Surely you find that more than just *interesting*?"

"It might be," Cerezzi said, easing his large frame onto the window sill and twining a cord from the window shade around one finger. "But then again it might not."

"Why not, Lieutenant?" asked Brenda, her eyes moving uneasily to Daniel.

"Well, for one thing, most murderers don't leave calling cards announcing their intentions."

"Exactly," Daniel said excitedly. "But this letter arrived anonymously."

"No, Rabbi. The letter is anonymous to you and me. But its contents, and the fact that it was handwritten, suggest that it was not anonymous to Wahl."

"I'll grant you that," Daniel said grudgingly. "But I still don't understand. Are you planning to ignore this letter?"

"No. I'm not going to do that either, Rabbi. We had a number of things to check before you brought this letter in. Now we have an additional job, to locate Myra Wahl's ex-boyfriends." Cerezzi laughed out loud, flashing large white teeth. "I've been a cop now twenty-six years, in homicide almost twenty. I've checked out plenty of boyfriends in plenty of murder cases. But this is the first time I ever went looking for a rabbi's boyfriends."

"Lieutenant," said Daniel, his face stiffening. "I don't thing you're taking this seriously enough. I intend to follow this up."

"What are you planning, Rabbi?"

"To find the writer of this letter. You see," and he made no effort to restrain his sarcasm, "unlike you, I believe this letter is critical."

"A word of advice, Rabbi." A new tone crept into Cerezzi's voice. "If your theory is correct, the writer of this letter is dangerous. And will have no hesitation about killing. You follow?"

Daniel gave a barely perceptible nod.

"A second word of advice. If your theory is incorrect, the writer of this letter will probably not be too pleased that you read it. And will be less pleased if you accuse him of murder. In fact, might even slap you with a lawsuit."

"Thanks for the warning." Abruptly, Daniel headed for the door, turning only to smile a farewell at Brenda. "I'll see you tomorrow, Brenda."

"Are you and the rabbi good friends?" Cerezzi asked casually, when the door had closed on Daniel.

"We're acquaintances. Lieutenant, do you really think the letter is so inconsequential?"

"Not at all." Cerezzi picked up the note and reread it, shaking his head. "Something about this letter is damned interesting. Let's check it out for prints—although I'm sure your friend the rabbi's are all over it—and get our graphologist to take a look at it."

"So why did you act so unconcerned?"

"Because that guy is a rabbi, not a cop. I don't care for amateurs mixing in police investigations."

"I hate to tell you, but I think this time your strategy backfired. All you did was convince Daniel that unless he took it seriously, nobody would."

"Them's the breaks, as we used to say in Brooklyn. Besides, I did what I had to, which was to warn him to watch his step. But that fellow's pretty determined. Who knows, maybe he'll come up with something."

"And maybe he'll get himself killed. You gave me the shivers, Joe, when you gave him that warning. I don't want anything to happen to him."

"Sure you two are just acquaintances?"

Briefly, Brenda recounted how the rabbi had recovered her stolen watch.

"Different from the rabbis I remember seeing as a kid," Cerezzi teased. "By the way, we still have no real alibi for him for last night, do we?"

"No."

"Maybe the rabbi and I should have another talk. I can see how it might be easier for me to press him than for you."

Cerezzi strolled over to Brenda's desk. He lifted the bottle of roses and inhaled theatrically.

"Beauties. Don't often see roses in homicide. Who gave them to you?" Brenda's flush deepened. "The acquaintance?" Cerezzi's eyes twinkled as he walked out.

Monday Evening

After dinner, Daniel drove the short distance to the Holiday Inn where the Wahls were staying. He had intended to go straight to their room, but as he went through the revolving doors, he felt his courage deserting him. What could he say to this man and woman whose daughter had been murdered less than twenty-four hours earlier? Once, during his first year in the rabbinate, he had paid a condolence call to a couple whose twenty-year-old son had hanged himself in the family basement. That day he had walked around the block three times before he could summon the strength to go in. Now those same feelings swept over him again, and his stomach clenched into a tight knot. He let the door complete its revolution, and then he was outside again. This time one trip around the block sufficed. Ten minutes later, he reentered the hotel, found out the room number, and took the stairs to the third floor.

To his great relief, Reuben Rappaport answered his light knock. "It's good that you're here," Rappaport said softly in greeting and then turned to Sam and Betty Wahl and introduced him. "Rabbi Daniel Winter, a close friend and colleague of Myra's." Rappaport's relief was transparent—within minutes he was gone.

Daniel found himself facing an elderly couple who sat huddled on the bed, Sam Wahl with one arm around his wife.

"I suppose God doesn't take care of His own," Betty Wahl said quietly, breaking the silence that accompanied Rappaport's departure. When Daniel didn't respond, the woman went on. "She was a rabbi. You'd think God would protect a rabbi from being killed, wouldn't you?"

58

Daniel did not answer. He longed for inspiration, for words that could lessen this woman's agony. But when Rebecca had died he had learned that, for the bereaved, such words do not exist. Words could help, but only when death was long past, abstract. For this man and woman in front of him, no word could erase the one fact that did matter, that tomorrow they would bury their daughter.

"Tell me something, Rabbi," Betty Wahl said, her reddened eyes searching his face. "You believe in God?"

"Yes. I do."

"Give me one good reason!"

"Because your daughter devoted her life to being a rabbi, to bringing people to God and Judaism. If there is no God, then Myra wasted her life. I don't believe she did, Mrs. Wahl, and I don't think you believe that either."

Betty Wahl's heavily made-up face crumpled. She slumped, her body racked with sobs. For the first time since Daniel entered, Sam Wahl strung together an entire sentence.

"Forgive my wife, Rabbi. We're not atheists. We're just hurt."

The man's simple dignity broke Daniel's reserve, and he felt tears starting in his eyes.

Betty Wahl looked up, and there was a weak smile on her face.

"Of course I'm not an atheist. If I didn't believe in God, I wouldn't be angry at Him, would I? But why, Rabbi, does He allow such things to happen?" She emphasized the word "rabbi" as if the title conferred on Daniel exclusive inside information.

"If I knew God I'd be God," said Daniel, quoting a medieval Jewish philosopher who might well have been responding to the same question eight hundred years earlier.

"In other words, there is no reason?"

"Mrs. Wahl, if God were in this room, is there any reason He could give that would satisfy you? So what can I say? Only that God gave human beings free will and so He had to limit His own acts in the world. If every time a person raised his hand to hurt another, God stopped him, there would be no free will. And then we'd be no different from animals. Mrs.

Wahl, the person who killed your daughter last night was not sent by God to do so. It was he—not God—who decided to drive as he drove, and he who decided not to stop and help Myra after he struck her."

"You're a smart man, Rabbi. I can't answer you. But all that goes through my head is that one day ago my daughter was alive. And now she's gone forever."

Sam Wahl spoke again. A tall, striking, white-haired man, his resemblance to Myra was uncanny. His eyes held a dazed expression.

"Were you a close friend of Myra's?"

Daniel hesitated. "As a matter of fact, no."

His first instinct had been to say yes, a white lie that would hurt no one. But last night, thousands of people had heard Myra Wahl insult him. Sooner or later, someone would tell the Wahls about that. He wondered how they would react if they knew that just a few hours earlier the police had asked him to account for his movements last night.

"Your daughter didn't approve of me. At least of my attitudes on feminism. Over the years we had some vigorous disagreements. She once called me a male chauvinist piglet. Said I didn't have the stature to be a male chauvinist pig."

Betty Wahl's face brightened, tears shining through her crooked smile.

"That sounds like Myra."

"I moderate a radio show here in Los Angeles, *Religion and You*. Myra was the guest rabbi several times." The couple nodded. Bety's hand slipped over Sam's. "Last night we got into a bit of an argument. Myra was attacking something I'd written, and her attack got a little personal. After the show, she apologized. But I was so hurt or mad—both, I suppose—that I refused to accept her apology. I feel pretty bad about that, and now I'd like to do anything I can to help."

"You're feeling guilty, Rabbi?" Betty Wahl asked.

Daniel nodded.

"Don't. Myra was like that. When she'd get angry it was no holds barred. I used to tell her that she'd destroy the whole world for the sake of a good line in an argument." Her voice was calmer now. "My daughter was a good person. It wasn't for herself that she'd get angry. It was for other people or for an ideal. After she'd explode she'd always regret it. She didn't go around hating people."

Daniel shifted uncomfortably, then took out a copy of the note from his pocket. It was smaller now. He had cut off all but the first two lines.

"Last night Myra left a copy of my book at the radio station. I was looking at it this afternoon. There was a note inside that she had apparently used as a bookmark. It's probably not relevant to what happened, but it caused me to wonder." He cleared his throat. "Do you know of any boyfriends with whom Myra might have had an unpleasant breakup?"

A nervous look passed between the couple. Somehow Daniel detected fear on their faces. There was silence in the room. Then Betty Wahl spoke, stiltedly.

"I don't think there was any special young man in her life. I suppose soon there would have been. But until now she was too caught up in her professional obligations."

"I want to show you this note. I know it's a long shot, but could you tell me if the handwriting looks familiar?" Sam Wahl bent over his wife's shoulder and they read the expurgated text. "No one will ever love you as I have loved you."

Betty Wahl's cry was like a startled animal's. Her husband's hand griped her arm.

"I knew that bum would never let Myra go," said Betty, fiercely. The note trembled in her hand.

"Who?" Daniel asked. "Who wrote it?"

"I'd know that handwriting anywhere," she said. "When Myra was home two summers ago a letter arrived every day."

"From who?"

"Evelyn Rand, Myra's roommate in New York."

As Daniel had driven home, his mind had been in turmoil. The elderly couple had given Daniel their daughter's old New York phone number. He suspected that the scarcity of available apartments in Manhattan made it likely that Evelyn Rand still lived in the same place. But should he call her—confront her over the telephone? He looked at his watch. 9:25.

It was now well past midnight in the East. I'd certainly catch her unawares, he thought. Or should he break his word and contact the police? Thirty-five years of good citizenship training and his first instinct told him he should transmit all information in a criminal case to the police. But when he had lifted the hotel phone, Sam Wahl had clamped an unexpectedly strong grip on his arm. His pale eyes were pleading.

"Don't call the police, Rabbi."

"Why not?"

"Because it won't bring out daughter back."

"Of course it won't, Mr. Wahl. But the author of this," and he lifted the note, "might have murdered your daughter. Don't you want her caught?"

The man's face was drained.

"At what cost, Rabbi? Our daughter is dead. But at least her name is safe. But if you go to the police there'll be an investigation. Maybe Evelyn Rand is guilty, maybe not. But either way, everybody's going to find out that she . . . had an affair with out daughter. We've known for a long time what went on between Myra and that woman—it is the greatest shame of our lives. We used to live in panic that it would become known, and when Myra broke off with her it was like waking up from a nightmare. Now, if you go to the cops," his voice became bitter, "that note will 'be printed in every goddamn newspaper in the city."

"Rabbi," Betty Wahl's face was ashen, "we would never have spoken so openly with you if we thought you'd take this information to the police. It's only because you're a rabbi that we told you all these things—in confidence."

"And if Evelyn Rand is guilty you're going to let her get away?"

"We don't give a damn about Evelyn Rand." Betty Wahl stood up and moved toward him, her hands gesturing wildly. "But if this becomes known, you'll kill our daughter a second time. And what about us? Tell me, Rabbi, how will we lift our heads after everybody reads about Myra's lesbian lover?" The overwrought woman seemed to sense Daniel's lingering resistance. She gripped his arm. "Tell me, Rabbi, your parents, are they alive?"

"Yes."

"Well, imagine, just imagine, that you had had a homosexual relationship. And suddenly you were dead and a story circulated, not just in private, but in the newspapers about it, how would they feel?"

The question silenced Daniel.

Even then Daniel had persisted, but the soul had gone out of his argument. He succeeded, however, in extracting one major concession. He himself would investigate Evelyn Rand's movements, and if he found clear evidence that pointed to her as the murderer he could then go to the police. "By the way," he told the Wahls, "I've already given the police the original of this note."

"Well, they won't get any more information from us," Betty Wahl said, a sob in her voice. She looked at him. "Our daughter is dead, Rabbi. Please don't cause us any more pain."

Now, away from the grieving couple, every rational instinct he had told him to ignore their plea. But he couldn't— he had given his word. For now, at least, he had to go it alone.

Daniel unlocked his apartment door and went straight for the phone. He knew he'd better call immediately or he'd lose his nerve. He nervously punched out the numbers.

An answering machine came on after just one ring. And he was startled. For the last five hours he had focused so intently on the hatred in Evelyn Rand's note that he was totally unprepared for the warmth, even cheeriness, of the voice that now greeted him. "Hi. This is Evvie. Don't hang up. I know you're tempted. But don't. I'm out of town for a few days. But through the wonders of remote control I receive my messages daily. So please leave your name, telephone number, and any other pertinent information, and I will return your call as soon as possible."

"This is Daniel Winter. You don't know me, but it would be very much to your advantage if we speak immediately. I assure you that this is not a joke. Please call me at any hour." He listed his home and office numbers.

Only when he hung up did he realize that his forehead was beaded with sweat.

Tuesday Morning

At 10:45, Daniel walked through the elaborate pillars at the entrance to the Pico Boulevard Temple, struck, as always, by how different this majestic building was from his own simpler synagogue. Inside, the fifteen-hundred seat sanctuary was rapidly filling to a Yom Kippur size crowd. He started down the center aisle, and as he walked he sensed heads turning. A tinny woman's voice reached him: "He has some nerve showing up here." He turned to see the object of her comment. But there was no one behind him. Then he understood. He shrugged and walked straight ahead.

"Daniel," a voice called him, several rows from the back. He turned and saw a dark-haired man of medium height, sporting a perfectly trimmed mustache and stylish dark-rimmed glasses. Ronnie Gold. Gold patted the seat beside him with a mechanical smile. Daniel hesitated, but Gold beckoned again. There was no graceful exit. He squeezed past five pairs of knees and sat down miserably.

"Hello, Rabbi," said Gold, taking his hand in a firm grip. Daniel wondered if he were being mocked. Gold had no reason to call him by his title, since he and Daniel had been at the seminary together. For six months they had even been *havrutot*, learning together three hours Sunday through Thursday in preparation for their Talmud class. But their friendship did not survive their final year before ordination, when they both fell in love with the same girl.

Leah Mason. The slender black-haired girl with the olive skin and clear blue eyes. It was Daniel who had dated her first, all during the fall and the early winter. In their circles, this should have been enough time to know. Leah claimed she was certain by the third date that she wanted to become Mrs. Winter. But Daniel was unsure. Not then. And not in mid-January either, when Leah delivered her ultimatum. He loved Leah. She was a Yeshiva boy's fantasy—beautiful, brilliant, and passionately Jewish. Most of all, he liked her intellectual feistiness. She was different from the other women he had dated who sat and listened quietly to his endless, well-reasoned, and dogmatic theories about the world.

But she also frightened him. For Leah Mason, he knew, was more intelligent that she was good. And she was ambitious. She wanted to be Mrs. Winter. That was fine, but her plans for Mr. Winter were more ambitious than a career in the pulpit. She argued eloquently for the options—law, writing, psychology—in all of which Daniel had talent and in all of which he was interested. She loved Daniel fiercely and wanted to marry him, but *only* on her terms. Just as, he ruefully admitted to himself, he wanted her on his. After weeks of painful indecision, he asked for a half-year break in their relationship. Then he'd know, he said.

It was during those six months that Ronnie Gold made his move. Though a rabbinical student, Gold had no intention of taking a pulpit. In his family it was a tradition for the men to study in Yeshiva until their mid-twenties and then go into the family business. That business, The Golden Table, was one of the largest wholesale furniture distributors on the East Coast. Gold pursued Leah with his charm, his total devotion, and the determination of the very rich boy who was accustomed to getting everything he wanted.

He got Leah. But it would be Ronni Gold's curse that he was never sure why. Was he the love of Leah Mason's life as she was of his? Or was he simply the most attractive alternative after Daniel Winter?

When Daniel was not invited to the wedding, he understood.

Ten years later, Daniel had moved to Los Angeles, where Gold had established and now directed the West Coast operation of The Golden Table. Not long after, Leah invited the recently widowed rabbi to their home for dinner.

After that, Daniel was often a guest at the Golds for Sabbath dinner. At first it had been very pleasant between the three of them, but then the atmosphere grew progressively more strained. And then abruptly Ronnie Gold made it clear—very clear—that Daniel Winter was no longer to be a part of their lives. The invitations ceased. From then on, Daniel's few encounters with Gold had been characterized by a labored politeness on both sides.

Now, Daniel thought nervously, Ronnie seemed altogether too eager for Daniel's company.

"I didn't even know you knew Rabbi Wahl," Daniel spoke first, wishing to control the conversation's direction.

"As a matter of fact, Myra and I were second cousins. We had virtually no contact. But naturally, I came to the funeral."

"Where is Leah?" Daniel hesitated before asking, then decided it would sound less natural if he didn't mention her at all.

"Previous engagement. . . . Oh, by the way, have you heard the rumor?"

Daniel shook his head.

"Something about Myra's death being no accident." Gold's voice was elaborately casual; his eyes were on the crowd.

Daniel said nothing. He was conscious of the faint, musky aroma of the aftershave Gold wore.

"You and Myra had a bit of a to-do Sunday night, didn't you?"

"I didn't know you listened to the show."

"I don't. As a matter of fact, I was out of town on Sunday." Gold's dark eyes stared keenly at him. "Big fight I heard you two had."

"Who told you that?" Daniel's voice was a little too loud. Don't get paranoid, he cautioned himself.

Gold gestured with his ringed hand. "Lots of people here mentioned it. Don't worry. But you know cops. They'll probably want to know where you were, seeing as Myra got killed so shortly after your . . . disagreement." His stare seemed to pierce Daniel's forehead. "I suppose you can tell them where you were, right?"

"Right," Daniel replied. Turning aside, he saw with relief that the service was about to start.

Rabbi Rappaport mounted the pulpit. His thick fingers grasped the curtain covering the Torah ark and he brought it to his lips and kissed it. He turned toward the congregation and in a slow cadence read the twenty-third psalm. "The Lord Is my Shepherd."

Then he began, "Myra Wahl was a modern Deborah, leading the Jewish people against our enemies, indeed against all enemies of justice." He went on to describe "this noble soul who challenged the sexism of the Judaism she loved, and by becoming a rabbi proved that Judaism could accommodate itself to a world in which women are equal. Indeed I don't know," and here his voice started to break, "if I was *her* equal."

Loud sobs could be heard, merging into a wail, inside the immense hall of the synagogue. Myra Wahl's death, Daniel reflected sadly, had succeeded in provoking a display of love which had been denied her in her lifetime.

Irv Burnside, the synagogue treasurer, who had bluntly advised Myra to resign at the Sunday meeting, was not among those who wept. Burnside prided himself on not being a hypocrite. His presence at the funeral was the one concession he'd make to public opinion. Listening to Rappaport, he fantasized about what would happen if the rabbi, or he himself for that matter, said what they really thought. "Myra Wahl was a pain in the neck. Of course she did not deserve to die, and what happened to her is terrible, but that's no reason to delude ourselves into thinking she was a saint." Does Rappaport believe his lies, he wondered? Because there was one thing Irv Burnside was damn sure of—if Myra Wahl were resurrected, it would take no more than forty-eight hours to fire her again.

A man with an aquiline nose, almost bald, rose to speak next. His mouth was set in a tight line, and he stepped forward with an air of authority. Daniel looked questioningly at Ronnie Gold. "Milton Karp," Gold said. "President of the temple. He and I sit together on the Jewish Federation's appropriations committee."

The voice up front sounded hoarse behind the microphone. "It was my privilege to bring Myra Wahl to the Pico Boulevard Temple. . . ."

Another funeral hagiography, Daniel thought, his eyes scanning the temple. Brenda was easy to locate. She was seated in the front row, two seats away from Sam and Betty Wahl. He did not envy her.

After Karp concluded his brief talk, the cantor sang the *El Malei Rakhamim*, the memorial prayer asking "God, who is full of compassion," to bind the soul of the dead in the bond of eternal life. The entire congregation stood while Rappaport led them in the kaddish prayer.

The crowds began to file out.

"Going to the burial?" Gold asked Daniel casually, as they stood up.

Daniel glanced at his watch. "I can't. I'm just too rushed." He wove his way through the crowded aisle. Inside the synagogue, the atmosphere was stifling. He regretted missing the burial, but when he thought of the rest of his day he could barely suppress a groan. Radio show at two and a meeting at Cerezzi's request on God knows what at four. But the thought of the late dinner with Brenda cheered him.

He drove back to his synagogue quickly; the traffic was light. Five calls had come in.

"I'm in a rush," he told Pat. "Any urgent ones?"

"Two. You've procrastinated for two weeks deciding if you'll speak at the sisterhood meeting. The invitations have to be printed tomorrow, and Jeanne Rosenstein needs an answer, pronto."

He glanced at his pocket calendar.

"That's the fourth, right?"

"Uh-huh."

"Okay, I'll do it. Do me a favor though, Pat. You call Jeanne. Tell her I'll speak on 'Where have all the young Jews gone?'"

He started into his office.

"There was another message," Pat followed him. "A woman. She said the urgency was from your end. Sounded mysterious." She glanced at her notes. "Evelyn Rand."

Daniel grabbed the note out of Pat's hand. He looked at it and then gave a loud exclamation, his hand against his forehead.

"What's wrong?" she asked him.

"I can't believe it, Pat. You forgot to get the area code on this call."

She looked at him in mock exasperation.

"What are you talking about? She's here in Los Angeles. At the Century Plaza."

Daniel raced into his office and dialed. "Room 324," he requested, looking at the message. The extension was picked up almost immediately.

"Is this Evelyn Rand?"

"Yes."

"This is Daniel Winter."

In the ensuing seconds of silence. Daniel became painfully aware that he had evolved no strategy for dealing with Evelyn Rand. One thing was clear, though. He'd have to drop the rabbinic persona.

"Do you know why I'm calling, Ms. Rand?"

"No."

"I think you do."

He let the statement rest. Silence.

"Could you please tell me what brings you to Los Angeles?"

"Listen. I've been acting respectfully because when I called your office I found out that you are a rabbi. But my patience is starting to run thin."

"I think we should meet. Today."

"Why?"

"To discuss the murder of Myra Wahl."

He heard her indrawn breath. When she spoke again her voice belied the calmness of her words. "No. I see no reason for us to meet. In fact, I will thank you . . ."

"Before you hang up, Ms. Rand," and quite suddenly, Daniel felt in control, "let me offer you a second reason you and I should talk. To discuss a letter I'm holding. It's about two and a half weeks old. Written in remarkably short proximity to her death. Is that reason good enough for you?"

She agreed to meet him at six P.M.

Tuesday Afternoon

"This is Daniel Winter, substituting for Dick Stevens, and it's time for *Dialogue*." Five seconds of music followed.

"Sunday night, two hundred and fifty thousand of you listened to *Religion and You* here on KLAX. An hour after the show, one of the evening's panelists, Rabbi Myra Wahl, was killed by a hit-and-run driver. Police believe that the killing was intentional.

"This was not the only homicide in Los Angeles on that day. That same night, a housewife was strangled, most likely during the course of a robbery, and a sixteen-year-old girl was knifed in an alleyway.

"Three brutal murders in one day.

"There is one thing we can be sure of—*if* the murderers of these three women are caught, they will pay a far smaller price than that which they exacted from their victims. The average murderer convicted in California serves ten to fifteen years before being paroled.

"But am I right in assuming that you share with me the desire for tougher measures against violent criminals? Why don't you call up so that I can hear what you're thinking and so that we can dialogue."

The monitor was quickly filling.

"Hello, Jennifer, you're on the air."

"The murderer will pay a far smaller price . . ." Jennifer started, mimicking Daniel's statement. "Those are just code words, aren't they? What you're really saying is that you believe in capital punishment." There was a pause. "Well—do you?" she demanded.

"Yes . . . in certain cases."

"I'm surprised, Daniel. I really am. I listen to *Religion and You* every week, and I always thought you were a religious man."

"I like to think I am."

"Then how can you advocate disobeying the Bible—'Thou shalt not kill'?"

"There's no such verse in the Bible."

"What?"

"'Thou shalt not kill' is a mistranslation. In the original Hebrew, the sixth of the Ten Commandments reads, *Lo tirtzakh*—thou shalt not murder. The Bible forbids murdering, which means killing an innocent person."

"That's ridiculous. Are you telling me the Bible sanctions killing?"

"Jennifer, are you married?"

"Yes, though I hardly see the relevance—"

"Just hang in there a minute. If men broke into your home and wanted to murder your husband, and the only way to stop them would be to kill them, would you?"

"Yes. But that's not killing, that's self-defense."

"It's called killing in self-defense, and killing in self-defense is the kind of killing the Bible allows."

"Do you think, Daniel, the Bible would consider it self-defense to strap a powerless ex-murderer into an electric chair?"

"In the Bible, capital punishment is legislated so 'that people should see and be afraid.' In other words, capital punishment is society's self-defense against murderers."

"But it's been proven repeatedly that capital punishment does not deter."

"That's not true. . . ."

Jennifer's call established the tone of the show. In the next fifty minutes twelve calls came in on the death sentence—seven in favor, five against—and all of them passionate. Midway through the hour Daniel announced that he was activating the Scrambler, hoping to prompt calls from those too shy to go on the air otherwise. The next caller's voice did indeed sound unfamiliar, but when he said "raison d'être" and "ergo," in the same sentence, Daniel knew it had to be Eddie Schwartz, a long-standing member of his congregation, who called *Religion and You* at least once a month. "Raison d'être" and "ergo" insinuated themselves into every one of his calls. Not even the Scrambler can disguise Eddie, Daniel thought with amusement.

At 1:58 the engineer gave him the two-minute warning.

"Maybe one of you listening right now knows something about Myra Wahl's death that the police should know. Maybe you saw something that evening that you now realize has a greater significance than you previously thought. If you know anything at all, please come forward. Call 658-7511 and ask for Lieutenant Joe Cerezzi or police psychologist Brenda Goldstein. If you are uncomfortable calling the police, then I offer myself as an intermediary. Call me at my office, 204-5681." He repeated both numbers. "Please come forward. Let's start defeating crime, one murder at a time. Thank you."

His heart was still pounding when Bartley Turner walked into the studio. He grabbed Daniel's hand and pumped it several times.

"We're gonna do business together, Danny boy. You're a natural. Confrontational, but not obnoxious. And that announcement at the end." Bartley Turner kissed the tips of his fingers. "Mmmm, that was genius. Human interest, just what people love."

Daniel was quiet, but this went unnoticed by Turner. He pulled Daniel by the arm. "Come on, Ashley wants to see you now."

Daniel had met Ashley Carter, general manager of KLAX, only three or four times, yet each time he was struck by the fact that such a taciturn individual was running a talk-show station. Now, to Daniel's surprise, Carter's handshake was as effusive as Bartley Turner's. Within seconds, he got down to business.

"I just spoke with our affiliate station in Chicago. They confirmed a deal that's been in the works for several weeks. Dick Stevens is going there next month. We want you to take over *Dialogue*."

Daniel's mouth opened, and then shut again.

"I hope that's a yes you're trying to get out," Turner teased, winking at Carter.

Daniel finally found his voice.

"I'm flattered. I really am. But what about my congregation—could I do both?"

"We've given that a lot of thought, Daniel, and we don't think it would be wise. We're hiring you because we believe you can become a major voice in American life. If you're also known as a clergyman, people will react to you differently. You know, they'll think they always have to speak with you on a religious plane, like that Jennifer who called today. Or they'll be inhibited or too respectful. No," Carter shook his head, "it wouldn't be in your best interest. Besides, Daniel, realistically, would your congregation allow it?"

Daniel shook his head resignedly. On more than one occasion, Wilbur Kantor and the executive committee had expressed their unhappiness over his radio show and his active schedule of outside lectures. "We're paying you a full-time salary, Rabbi," Kantor had once said. "Doesn't that entitle us to a full-time rabbi?" "But I am full-time," Daniel had replied, and proceeded to prove, though unfortunately only to his own satisfaction, that he fulfilled all his responsibilities to the synagogue, that the radio show and the lectures were on his own time, and that, anyway, they added to the stature of the congregation. Kantor and the board were not persuaded. Full-time for a rabbi, Daniel came to realize, did not mean forty hours a week. What the board wanted was an assurance that he was always available, that he had no priorities aside from the job. Just last month, Seymour Raff, a synagogue vice-president, had suffered a heart attack, and when his wife, Martha, called Daniel to come to the hospital she was told that he was speaking at a conference in St. Louis. Now Martha Raff was furious with him, and Seymour was hurt that the rabbi had not visited him in the hospital until two days later. No, the congregation would not allow it. It would be absurd to even raise the issue with them.

Carter handed him a sheet.

"Look at the figure on that paper, Daniel. I suspect you won't suffer by coming to work with us." The math was easy.

For two hours of talk-show hosting five days a week, KLAX was offering forty percent more than what the synagogue paid him.

"But it's not a question of money, Ashley. I have a commitment there. I can't just walk out."

"We understand that, and we're willing to accommodate you. Until the synagogue finds a replacement, you go on fulfilling your pastoral obligations. They'll find a new man in a month or two." Carter paused, leaned forward, and placed both palms on the desk. "Daniel, we think you're the right man. But we need an answer soon."

"How soon?"

"Ideally, today. But I can let you have up to five days."

"That's impossible," Daniel said. "You're asking me to leave the rabbinate. I don't know what I'm going to say, Ashley, but I need more time."

"A week at the outside, Daniel. No more. If you can't do it, we'll have to find someone else. But you're our first choice." He looked sharply at Daniel. "I don't know if you appreciate what an opportunity you're being offered."

I should be ecstatic, Daniel thought grimly, as he left the meeting. But he wasn't. Had Carter insisted on an immediate answer he had no idea what he would have said.

Now he had time. One week. But what then? What would be clear in seven days that wasn't clear now? He closed his eyes. Too much was happening: Myra's murder just after their quarrel, the police suspecting him, Evelyn Rand's note, meeting the Wahls . . . too much.

He looked at his watch. Time for the meeting with Cerezzi. I should be ecstatic, he thought again. He laughed once, bitterly.

Daniel arrived at Cerezzi's office fifteen minutes early for his four o'clock appointment. The lieutenant was not in, but his three-thirty appointment was waiting in the outer office—a man in his early forties, about six feet, without a trace of fat on his body. He was badly in need of a shave.

"Hello," Daniel said, "I'm . . ."

"Daniel Winter," the man filled in. The man gave a small

smile. "I have a thing about voices. Hear them once and never forget 'em. And your voice I've certainly heard more than once. You're a big radio personality."

Daniel smiled at the stardom conferred on him.

"My wife was a big fan of yours. As a matter of fact, yours might have been the last voice she ever heard."

The smile froze on Daniel's face.

"What do you mean? Who are you?"

"Elmer Brine," the man said.

"Your wife was the woman murdered Sunday night?" Brine nodded. "Oh, I'm so sorry, Mr. Brine."

Brine cleared his throat and stared down at his hands. "When I got home Sunday night it was late, after one A.M. Elaine, that's my wife, was lying on the floor. The radio was still on, loud. Who knows, maybe the killer turned it up to drown out the murder. Anyway, it was tuned to KLAX. And then when the coroner said she was killed about eleven, I figured she must have been listening to your show. She tried never to miss it."

"Have the police made any headway?" Daniel said, wishing to change the subject.

"Nope. And I don't think they're likely to. You know what they say—if the cops don't catch a killer inside of forty-eight hours, there's a good chance they never will. Well, it's almost forty-eight hours, and I'm the only one they're questioning. It's damned unfair.'" The last three words exploded.

"What is, Mr. Brine?"

"That I loved my wife, and she's gone now. And that Cerezzi is demanding that I account for all of my movements on Sunday. That *I* should be suspected."

Daniel found himself empathizing. What would it have been like if when Rebecca had died the police had started questioning him? He wanted to comfort or at least to calm the man before Cerezzi spoke to him.

"Maybe this sounds ridiculous, but you shouldn't take it personally. I'm sure this kind of thing is routine police procedure after a homicide. They question everyone."

"You don't know what you're talking about. Cerezzi's *after* me. Listen, Mr. Winter, I don't know what you're here for, but lemme give you one word of advice. When the cops ask you something, tell 'em the truth. *But don't volunteer anything.* You think you're just being helpful. But next thing you know—" He stopped abruptly as footsteps approached. Elmer Brine's frightened scenario had not prepared Daniel for the genial smile Lieutenant Joe Cerezzi flashed as he walked in.

"Sorry for the delay, gentlemen." He turned to Daniel. "I'll be with you as soon as possible, Rabbi."

Cerezzi showed the tall Brine into his office. Alone, Daniel wondered if the man's diatribe had been overheard. Brine had succeeded in stirring up a paranoia about cops that Daniel didn't know he had. He found himself examining the room for hidden microphones and wondering if the mirrors were one way. Was Cerezzi purposely late, hoping to provoke just this sort of reaction? He shivered involuntarily. Catch hold of yourself, he thought. He sat down, took a deep breath, and slowly counted to ten. . . .

It seemed only minutes later that Cerezzi opened his door, ushering Brine out.

"Good to see you again, Rabbi." Cerezzi's greeting was cordial, making Daniel ashamed of his earlier panic. "Brenda Goldstein tells me I was a bit hard on you yesterday. If so, I apologize. By the way," the lieutenant went on, motioning Daniel to take a seat, "any luck with that note?"

"No." It bothered Daniel to be less than truthful, particularly with a police officer. But then he rationalized that he had, after all, answered Cerezzi's question literally—so far he had not had any luck with the note.

"Still think it's the key to the murder?" Cerezzi smiled.

"I'm a rabbi, Lieutenant, not a policeman. Does it really matter to you what I think?"

"You're being prickly again, Rabbi. As a matter of fact I am quite interested in what you think. Brenda Goldstein told me how you recovered her stolen watch. I was impressed. Maybe it's a technique the burglary division should try. You sounded like a different sort of rabbi."

Daniel relaxed enough to allow himself a grin.

"With a name like Cerezzi I wouldn't imagine you've known too many rabbis."

"Oh, you'd be surprised. I grew up in Brooklyn, in Williamsburg. There was a synagogue right next to our apartment house, and I was the 'shabbes goy.' I'd turn off the lights Friday night. In the winter, I'd come in early Saturday morning to put on the heat. It was a very Orthodox congregation. Hasidim." Daniel nodded. "You're not Orthodox, I gather?"

"Why do you say that?"

Cerezzi patted his own balding head. "No yarmulke."

"Well, you're wrong. I am Orthodox. Just more liberal than the crowd you knew in Brooklyn. The yarmulke is more of a custom than a law; it's not really required all the time. And I figured it would be no great sanctification of God's name for me to be seen walking round homicide headquarters wearing a yarmulke."

"So your congregation is Orthodox?"

"As a matter of fact, no. I'm an Orthodox rabbi in a Conservative congregation with Reform laypeople."

Cerezzi chuckled. "I get the picture. You're a religious guy working with a bunch of Jewish goyim." The lieutenant's smile was infectious.

"That's a little unfair. But for an Italian cop you understand Jewish life pretty well. You know, so far this meeting has been a lot more pleasant than I expected. But I have a sneaking suspicion you didn't call me down here to discuss Jewish theology."

Cerezzi cleared his throat and shuffled the papers on his desk.

"Rabbi, a murder investigation takes us in many unexpected directions. When the perpetrator isn't an obvious one, we find ourselves checking out anybody with a declared animosity against the victim. I presume I'm not shocking you when I tell you that you fall into that category."

"What do you know about Myra Wahl and me?" Daniel asked, carefully keeping his tone conversational.

"That Rabbi Wahl insulted you on a live radio program. Called you a Nazi. I don't have to be a Jew to understand how much anger that might provoke. Even more interesting, after the show, she asked your forgiveness, and you refused it. Clearly she'd made you damned angry."

"You have a good system of informers," Daniel said bitterly. "One in particular."

Cerezzi's face was unperturbed. "Then I find out that you didn't get home till after one A.M. I think I have a right to know where you were, Rabbi. Do you agree?"

Daniel gave Cerezzi a long, measured look.

"Are you good at keeping secrets, Lieutenant?"

"Yes."

"Well, so am I. Sunday night I had an unexpected meeting. It's vital that meeting be kept secret."

"Were confidences revealed to you as a rabbi?"

His voice was almost a whisper, "No."

"You're making this hard for me, Rabbi. I have no desire to pry into your private life. It doesn't make a damn bit of difference to me what your meeting Sunday night was about. But I do need to confirm with that party that you were with them when Myra Wahl was killed. *Fahrshtein?*"

"I can't tell you who I met with, Lieutenant. To own up to a midnight meeting with me would put that individual in great difficulty."

Cerezzi raised an eyebrow. "Was it a woman, Rabbi? A married woman, maybe?"

"I don't want to talk about this anymore."

"Who are you protecting, Rabbi Winter, the woman or yourself?"

"I've already said more than I intended to say." Daniel got up to leave. "I gather I'm still free to go?"

Cerezzi waved his right hand in a gesture of dismissal.

"You realize that I'm going to hound you till I get the truth. You have no plans to be out of Los Angeles soon, do you?"

"No."

"That's fine, Rabbi. We'll be talking again, you and I."

Tuesday Evening

Daniel pushed open the doors of the Century Plaza. He wore a red yarmulke, the agreed-upon mark of identification. When no one approached him immediately, he surveyed the hotel lobby. In the right corner, a plain young woman, overweight, had flopped into a chair, a magazine on her knee. He walked past her twice. No reaction. A moment later, he felt a tap on his right shoulder. "Hello, Rabbi Winter."

He pivoted, barely disguising his surprise. Evelyn Rand was very different from the woman he had pictured. This woman was strikingly pretty, with light blue eyes, and shimmering strawberry-blond hair that cascaded softly to her shoulders. She wore a deep blue dress that emphasized her figure.

"Hello, Rabbi Winter," she repeated. Her voice was gentle.

Daniel felt his whole manner softening. Careful, he warned himself, she might be a murderer. He motioned her to follow him, and they walked over to two armchairs in the far corner of the lobby. Around them, the chairs were empty, but there were escalators in back of them, with a constant stream of people gong up and down.

"Don't you think we would be more comfortable in a more private setting?" Evelyn Rand asked, with a slightly nervous smile.

"Until a few things are cleared up, I'll be more comfortable right here. Okay?" He smiled at her, but the smile did not reach his eyes.

"Listen," she spoke, "there are a few things I want to ask . . ."

"No," Daniel broke in coldly, "I came here to ask questions, not to answer them. And I know enough about you, Ms. Rand, to put me in quite a strong bargaining position."

She glared at him, then nodded almost imperceptibly.

"Now, perhaps you could begin by telling me why you are in Los Angeles?"

"I'm in my last year of law school. Two firms brought me out for interviews."

"Name them!"

She did, and feeling somewhat foolish, Daniel jotted down the information. Pointless, he thought. Obviously it's going to check out. Why should she lie about things that could be so easily verified? What did he know about questioning murder suspects? He recalled Cerezzi's amusement.

"And you flew out here when?"

"Saturday morning. I wanted to be rested when the interviews started on Monday."

He took a copy of the note from his jacket pocket and passed it to her.

Her face blanched. "What are you, a rabbi or a blackmailer?" Hysteria was creeping into her soft voice.

"Let me tell you what I think happened," he said. "I think you loved Myra Wahl. And when she ended her relationship with you, you started to hate her. Obsessively. And so you wrote her that letter. And Sunday night, you killed her."

"I didn't kill her. I swear it. I loved Myra. I never stopped loving her."

Daniel pointed to the note. She crumpled it into her hand. "That's an odd way of showing it."

"I was angry. What do you expect? Myra ended our relationship so suddenly, of course I was angry. I wanted to hurt her, I'll admit that. But don't you understand, it was because I loved her—if she only told me she loved me, all my anger would have ended. I would have forgiven her anything if only she would have loved me again. Don't you understand what I'm saying?"

"I understand very well," said Daniel, steeling himself against a sudden rush of pity. "You were obsessed with Myra Wahl. You couldn't let her go. When you got out to LA maybe you even contacted her. I don't know. But somehow she made it clear, once and for all, that it was over. And so you killed her. Better she be dead than with someone else," His voice was cold. "Isn't that what really happened?"   .

"No," she shouted. Heads swiveled in their direction from the other end of the lobby. "Oh, please," she whispered, her voice strangled, "let's get out of here."

"I can't trust you," Daniel said. "We're staying right here, in public." He pulled the note out of her hand. "'I will not forgive,'" he read aloud. Then he looked at her. "Two weeks after you wrote that note, Myra Wahl was murdered. What would you think, Ms. Rand, if you were me?"

"I don't know." Her shoulders sagged. "Maybe I'd think just what you're thinking. But then I'd be wrong, too. As soon as I mailed that letter I realized it was wrong. But what could I do?"

"You could have called Myra up and apologized."

"I was afraid to speak with her."

Daniel gave a short laugh. "You write her a threatening letter, and you're the one who's afraid? Tell me, Ms. Rand, exactly what were you afraid of?"

Evelyn Rand spoke softly.

"I was afraid to make myself vulnerable to her again. I couldn't just call up, apologize, and hope that would be it. We would have spoken, and before I knew it, an hour would have gone by and I'd be hooked all over again." She threw down her hands in a gesture of despair. "Oh, it's pointless—you don't understand anything."

"Did you love her enough to kill her for leaving you?"

"No." Her voice started high, and she fought to control it. "I swear I didn't kill her."

"And if you had, would you admit it?"

She looked at him levelly. And made a decision.

"What I'm going to tell you now, I swear is the truth. And if it damages me, so be it. Sunday, I was going crazy thinking about Myra. It was bad enough in New York, but here I was in Los Angeles, in the same city with her. I wanted to speak with her. I needed to apologize for that horrible note, but most of all, I just needed to see her again. All day I resisted. I would pick up the phone, start dialing, and stop. I did everything to distract myself. I rented a car and went sight-seeing, watched television. Sunday evening I turned on the radio. I was flipping channels when I heard her voice. I couldn't believe it—I was sure I was going crazy. But it was her. I listened to your show straight through to the end. Then I drove over to her house. I figured I would meet her when she got back."

"What time was this?"

"I left the hotel about eleven forty-five. I wanted to be sure she'd be home when I got there."

"If you wanted to be sure, you would have left later. After all, Myra was jogging home."

"How was I supposed to know that?"

"Because I announced it on the air."

"Not when I was listening."

"Okay," Daniel nodded. "Did you pass any joggers on the way?"

"I don't remember. I didn't pass Myra. That I'm sure of. I would have noticed her." She gave a ragged sigh. "I got to her place a few minutes after midnight. And I waited. I just sat there in my car."

"And when she didn't come, what did you think?" He bit his lip. He was beginning to dislike himself heartily.

"I was depressed. I figured she probably had somebody else, and that's where she'd gone." Evelyn Rand shook her head broodingly. "At one-thirty—I remember the time because I decided to give myself till one-thirty—I left. I drove by a police car and an ambulance on the way back. It never occurred to me that it was Myra. Then yesterday I saw it in the papers."

"How did you feel when you found out Myra was dead?"

"Mixed. I . . . know it sounds terrible, but part of me was happy." Her eyes measured his reaction.

"I thought maybe I could start living again. You see, I never could accept that it was really over between us. After all, she didn't leave me because she stopped loving me. It was because of her job, and," her shining eyes met Daniel's defiantly, "Judaism's bigotry against gays. All the time she was alive, I thought maybe she'd get sick of the rabbinate, that

she'd realize one day that no one will ever love her the way I
do, that maybe, maybe, she'd come back. That's one of the
reasons I never could get involved with anybody else. And
sometimes I'd think," her voice caught, and she rigidly
controlled it, "that if only she was dead, then I'd know it was
over, and my life could start again. But I didn't kill her. . . .
Now I keep thinking that if only she'd come back to life, I'd
give her up. I really think I would. She didn't deserve to die."

"Were you at the funeral this morning?"

"I was afraid to go. Her parents hated me so." Her hands
twisted in her lap. "You showed them the note, didn't you?"

"What makes you say that?"

"Because how else would you have known I wrote it?
They knew about us. They also knew my handwriting. Myra
told me that. When she'd stay at her parents, I'd have to
disguise my writing. You showed it to them, and they told you
about me. Isn't that what happened?"

Reluctantly, Daniel nodded.

"They probably think I killed Myra, don't they?" Her
voice had a weary flatness.

"They think it's a possibility."

She drew a sharp breath."

"Do the police have the note?"

"Yes."

"Then why haven't they contacted me?"

"They will," Daniel said.

"But you have and they haven't. Why?"

"Maybe they don't know your name yet."

"That makes no sense at all. They could get my name as
easily as you did."

Daniel did not answer. A bitter smile spread slowly over
Evelyn Rand's face.

"The Wahls won't tell the cops my name, will they?"

Daniel did not answer.

"Of course not," she said. "They wouldn't want to let the
cat out of the bag. Can you imagine Betty Wahl telling the cops
that her daughter was gay? God, did they hate that. And me

also." Her eyes swept Daniel's face assessingly. "What about you, Rabbi? Do you think I'm disgusting?"

"I didn't say that," he said gently.

"But you think it, don't you? Myra showed me the verses in the Old Testament. Gay people are abominations—isn't that what your Bible teaches?"

"The Bible considers the act very wrong. It doesn't advocate hating homosexuals."

"Like hell it doesn't! I was raised Catholic, and I know what the Old Testament says, that homosexuals should be put to death. What do you call that, if not hatred?"

Many answers shot through Daniel's mind, but none seemed appropriate. Should he explain to this obsessed and hurt woman that the Bible's ruling only applied to male homosexuality and not lesbianism? Because lesbianism entailed no act of genital intercourse the rabbis did not see it as a biblically punishable act. Would that in any way appease her? He knew it wouldn't. She would see the whole thing as condescending, that Judaism didn't even recognize the possibility of one women loving another sexually. Or maybe he should tell her what one of his Talmud teachers had explained to him, that the liberal dispensing of death sentences in the Bible, for thirty-six offenses in all, was in many cases not to be taken literally, but was only the Bible's way of indicating how abhorrently the act was regarded. "And how do we know that the Torah wanted to limit the occurrence of capital punishment?" Rabbi Elyakim Schwartz had asked in the characteristic Talmudic singsong. "Because it insisted that the death sentence be imposed only where witnesses were present, and never on the basis of circumstantial evidence. Consequently, the only one who qualified for a death sentence was one who purposely performed his act in the presence of witnesses, presumably to undermine society."

Should I tell her that, Daniel wondered, looking at the torment so transparent on her face. Too complex. And the bottom line is, even if Evelyn Rand's understanding of the Bible is not a hundred percent correct, it's close enough. The Bible did see homosexuality as an attack on the family, as unnatural and a sin. Daniel had never had particular trouble accepting that before. Only it was hard to look this woman in the face and say that. And so he said none of these things.

"And what does your Catholic Church teach?" he said.

"Oh, they're no better," Evelyn Rand answered. "But I'm not a Catholic anymore." With an odd shake of her head, she said, "Understand something, Rabbi. You know how many men I've slept with in my life?" She held up one finger.

"And that wasn't out of desire. I just wanted to see if I was missing anything. I'm happy I did it. I found out I wasn't."

"Did Myra feel the same way?"

"She could have," Evelyn Rand said. "I was the only woman she ever slept with, but she told me she loved me more than any man she'd ever known."

"Then why did she leave you?"

"She knew the synagogue would fire her if they found out, and . . ."

"And what?"

Evelyn Rand looked down at her hands. "And she thought what we were doing was wrong. I don't blame her for that. Growing up with Betty and Sam Wahl and then going on to rabbinical school, it would have been a miracle if she'd felt any different. Oh, Myra can talk tough, but the funny thing is, deep down she isn't—wasn't—so liberated at all. If she had been she wouldn't have left me. We'd still be in New York. And she'd be alive."

A tear splashed on her clenched hands. Looking almost irritated, she pulled a tissue from her purse and rubbed her eyes.

"Now tell me, Rabbi, do you believe I murdered Myra?"

"Only you know whether you did, Ms. Rand. But you should know that I have deposited all the information I have about you in an envelope, with instructions that it be opened if anything happens to me." As he spoke, it occurred to him that it would have been a damn good thing if he had done so.

"But that was before you met me. Look at me now, Rabbi, and tell me, do you believe I murdered Myra?"

He looked at her, taking in the pale, tear-stained face, the earnest gaze of her blue eyes, and the determined set of her mouth. In his ten years as a rabbi he had met all kinds of people, and many souls had been poured out to him. He liked to think he was a good judge of character. But most of the time he had no way of knowing if his instincts were correct. Now he was being asked to gamble—who knows, maybe his own life— on his ability to judge character.

"No," he spoke softly, "I don't think you killed her."

"Thank you," For the first time since they met, Evelyn Rand smiled.

Daniel took the elevator to the hotel garage to retrieve his car. He looked at his watch. Twenty minutes till he met Brenda for dinner. This time, he wasn't looking forward to their meeting.

En route to the restaurant he reviewed his conversation with Evelyn Rand. A Talmudic quote, or rather a variation of one, nagged at him. "If not her, who?"

Brenda glanced at her watch again: 8:05. I wish he would get here already, she thought. The mâitre d' of the Kosher Korner, LA's only exclusive Jewish restaurant, was at her side solicitously.

"Would Madame like to be seated?"

Brenda shook her head. "I'll wait, thank you."

For the second time, she stepped in front of the long mirror in the restaurant's foyer. The emerald green dress was striking against her red hair and unusually bright eyes. But will Daniel like it? She caught herself and laughed. I'm nervous as a schoolgirl, she thought. Her mind went back to that first encounter with Daniel. She had been so tense and distraught, and Daniel hadn't helped matters by being alternately reassuring and distant. It seemed like she had known him for so long—hard to believe it was only eight days ago.

She heard the restaurant door push open, and then Daniel walked into the mirror's view. Brenda smiled. Daniel Winter just escaped being handsome, with black hair that curled untidily over his forehead and deep blue eyes. It was the eyes that held her. They had a serious, intent expression, the expression of a man who knew what he wanted. Yet in a funny way he looked boyish, too, with his eager impatience, tousled hair, and slightly crumpled shirt.

She turned around and called out to him, a smile lighting up her face. There was no answering smile. Daniel greeted her politely and moved abruptly to the nearest table. His politeness continued right up to the moment they scanned the menu and ordered. Then, as the waiter moved away, he turned to her, his voice hard.

"So why do you want to se me, Brenda? Because you like me so much or because you want to question a suspect?"

"What's that supposed to mean?" Her face tensed and went pale.

"I think you know."

"Daniel, I have no idea what you're talking about."

"Really?" He made no effort to disguise his sarcasm, "Then please explain to me how Lieutenant Cerezzi learned that I was so furious with Myra Wahl on Sunday night that I refused to forgive her."

"You don't trust me, Daniel, do you?" she said softly.

"I did."

"And now?"

"How can I, Brenda?" His burst of anger had faded, and she saw that his eyes had a dead expression. "What did you have to tell him all that for? Do you really believe I could kill Myra?"

"Of course not. And I didn't give that information to Cerezzi." There was no response. "You don't believe me, do you?"

He hesitated and then shook his head, refusing to meet her eyes.

"That hurts, Daniel."

"And what you did, doesn't? You threw me right in the middle of a murder investigation."

"It wasn't me."

No reaction. Daniel poked at the tablecloth with a breadstick.

"If you want to go on being a fool," Brenda flared, "that's your privilege. And if you have some need to cast me as the heavy, I suppose that's your right."

"Psychology be damned." He slammed his fist on the

table. "That information came to Cerezzi from somebody. And if not you, who?"

Desperation swept over Brenda. Daniel's anger was wrong and unfair but, she had to admit, quite understandable. She wanted to tell him what really had happened. But Daniel wasn't the only one to whom she felt responsible. There was also her responsibility to the police department. She didn't need Cerezzi to tell her that it was wrong to apprise someone under investigation of the informant against them. Then she looked at the hurt in Daniel's face and made a decision.

"Will you stop and think for a minute about Sunday night? Was I the only person present when you stormed out on Myra?"

"No." His voice was puzzled. And after a minute, in an incredulous tone, "Joanne Short?"

Brenda fidgeted in her seat. She had done what she wanted to do, and now that she had accomplished it, she felt guilty.

"There were several witnesses, Daniel."

"Only three—you, Mary Kuluski, and Joanne Short. You tell me you didn't do it. Sister Mary, as you recall, was running to catch a red-eye to New York. Which leaves one person . . . Joanne Short. Right?"

"You said it, not me."

"Okay, okay, I understand," he said, brushing aside her disclaimer. "But then how did Cerezzi know I didn't get home till after one? Joanne Short couldn't have told him that."

"You have to understand the position I was in. Monday morning . . . a witness," said Brenda, "came in to see Cerezzi. That person told him about your fight with Myra, and of course he asked if there were other witnesses. Well, it shook Cerezzi up when the witness gave him my name—you know, the coincidence that I should have been there and knew you. He called me into his office and asked if I had left with you. I said no. Cerezzi commented that it was strange. I had come with you, so why didn't we leave together? I explained that you were upset and had asked to be alone. But he kept pressing me. So I told him that I had tried to phone you, but you weren't in." Daniel nodded, but said nothing. "I'm sorry, Daniel, but that's how it happened."

"I understand. It's just making things a little unpleasant." He attempted a smile.

Brenda was stymied. Before dinner she had had every intention of asking Daniel where he had been on Sunday night. She had intended to probe—it was for his own good, wasn't it? But now she was afraid to ask him. The peace they had achieved was too fragile.

"So it all goes back to Joanne Short," said Daniel bitterly. "That . . ." Apparently, he was still too much the rabbi in her presence to say the word he really felt, "Did she really think I murdered Myra? My God, that's what I just asked . . ." he broke off and started laughing brittlely.

"What's so funny?" asked Brenda.

"Nothing," he said.

The evening ended as it had begun. With politeness. And tension.

Wednesday Morning

When Cerezzi telephoned Brenda Goldstein's office, her secretary took the call. "Dr. Goldstein's not in, Lieutenant. She's downstairs in the file room."

Cerezzi took the elevator to the division's file room, the repository of all the homicide records. One person sat at each of the three tables in the room. He saw Brenda's head at the far table, bent low, red hair gleaming in the dusty light.

"Lady, you planning on becoming a detective?"

Startled out of her deep concentration, Brenda swung round. Her face looked drawn.

"It's the second anniversary of my parents' murder," she said, her voice so low he had to strain to catch it. Cerezzi looked down at the gray folder she had been studying. An eight-by-eleven photo showed the Kaplans lying dead on their living room floor. The next picture was a close-up of Ted Kaplan, tanned and smiling, with his shirt-sleeves rolled up, looking very much like his daughter.

"I come up here often," Brenda said. "Go over it, again and again. And today especially . . ."

Cerezzi snapped the file shut. "Brenda, stop this! You've got to stop torturing yourself."

She straightened her shoulders. Her green eyes were unflinching as they met his. "I'm not going to stop, Lieutenant, until we catch him." Cerezzi looked away. "Anyway, Lieutenant, what brings you down here?"

For a moment Cerezzi could not remember. When he spoke, his voice was distracted. "We've got the car that killed Myra Wahl."

"Great!" Conscious of the two policemen at the other tables, she lowered her voice. "Where'd you find it?"

Cerezzi motioned with a faint movement of his head at their audience. "Let's talk in my office."

She hesitated only a moment before following him.

"How'd you find the car?" Brenda asked, as she moved into the stuffed chair by his desk. Somehow, she was grateful for the distraction Cerezzi brought.

"We didn't. It was brought in by the owner." He located a sheet of paper from the jumble on his desk. "Orrin Lewis—12468 Esther Avenue."

"Is he the killer?"

Cerezzi shook his head. He lit a cigarette and exhaled the smoke slowly.

"Not unless he directed the car by remote control. Lewis and his wife were in Chicago from Saturday until yesterday afternoon." Brenda opened her mouth to speak. "Don't worry," he cut her off. "We went after his story with a vengeance. It all checks."

"So what do you figure happened?"

"What so often happens in hit-and-run cases—the vehicle was stolen. The Lewis' left the car in their driveway the whole time they were gone. That block of Esther is no more than a five-minute walk from where Wahl was killed."

"Anyone else have the keys to the car?"

"Their next-door neighbors, a couple in their late fifties, early sixties."

"Have they been questioned?"

"Of course. The Lewises travel a lot, and when they're away, these neighbors keep an eye on the house, look after the car, you know, start it up occasionally to keep the battery alive. Anyway, they weren't much help. They never even noticed that the car was missing. My guess is that the killer stole the car Sunday night and returned it right after the killing. He probably figured the damage to the car would not be discovered till the morning. But he lucked out because the car's owners were out of town. The only damage was to the front fender and headlight. Orrin Lewis himself didn't realize the car had been damaged till he took it out this morning to go to work."

"And you're sure this car's the one?"

Cerezzi stubbed his cigarette out into a paper cup. "Dick Phillips called me from the lab just before I came to get you. He hasn't written his report yet, but he's sure. The force of the impact ground some of the fibers of Wahl's clothing into the body work of the car."

Brenda shuddered. She was still not inured to the realities of homicide work.

"It doesn't make sense to me. You mean the killer just sauntered into their driveway and drove off with their car?"

"It's not as unusual as you think, Brenda. The thief saw no lights on in the Lewis house, walked into the driveway, and broke into the car. A good car thief can get into a car and start it in well under sixty seconds. That part I understand." He picked up a pen and pointed it at her. "There's only one thing that puzzles me."

"What's that?"

"Myra Wahl's death was not an accident. That Buick was aimed straight at her. That's what I can't figure out. Why steal a car just to murder Myra Wahl?"

Cerezzi got up from behind his desk, went over to the battered table by the window, and poured out two cups of coffee from the percolator. He put in two sugars for himself, one for Brenda. She took hers, half-smiling.

"Do I gather from all this that Daniel Winter's non-alibi is no longer disturbing you?"

"Are you asking for personal or professional reasons?" Cerezzi grinned.

"Cut it out, Joe. I'm serious."

He held out his hands, palms upward.

"I've been in homicide a long time. You get an instinct after a while. Don't get me wrong, Brenda. That guy *is* hiding something, but I don't think it's murder."

"How bad is it that he refuses to tell us where he was?"

"It pricks my curiosity, that's for sure. And when you're dealing with murder, instinct or no instinct, you come to dislike loose ends. But on the other hand. . . . Did you ever hear of Detective Ellis Parker?" Cerezzi was a criminal history buff and prided himself on solving murders using techniques learned from old masters.

"Ellis Parker was a genius," he went on, his eyes suddenly alight, without waiting for her response. "A real-life Sherlock Holmes. He investigated two hundred and thirty-six homicides in his career and solved two hundred and twenty-six. That record's even more remarkable when you realize that most of the time they only brought him the hard cases."

"Okay, Lieutenant," Brenda humored him, "what does this Parker have to teach us about our case?"

"Parker had a general rule—don't trust someone with an alibi."

"Come again!"

"That's right. He figured anybody who was Johnny-on-the-spot with an alibi might well be the perpetrator. After all, and especially if you live alone, how *often* would you have a verifiable alibi? Think about it."

He put down his mug.

"Parker once had a case at Fort Dix, in New Jersey. A soldier had been murdered and the corpse was buried. By the time they found the body, the victim had been dead three months. The investigators were going crazy. They had over a hundred suspects on the base, and only one had an alibi for the day the murdered guy disappeared. This bothered Parker: why the hell did this soldier remember what he'd been doing three months earlier? So he went to work on the alibi, and before you knew it, he broke the guy down and got a confession."

"Did Parker ever make it to chief of police?" Brenda said teasingly. Cerezzi's own ambitions were no secret in the department.

The lieutenant shook his head, chuckling. "No, are you kidding? Parker died in prison."

"What!"

"Detective Parker was not a humble man. That's what undid him. During the Lindburgh kidnapping he was miffed that the police investigators didn't consult him. When they arrested Bruno Hauptmann he got it into his head that the guy was innocent. Parker conducted his own investigation and concluded that the real kidnapper was a man named Paul Wendel. When nobody listened to him, he kidnapped Wendel and beat a confession out of him. When Parker turned Wendel and his confession over to the cops, the guy promptly withdrew it. Hauptmann was convicted, and Parker found himself behind bars on a kidnapping charge. He died in prison in 1940." He sighed and reached for another cigarette. "What a waste."

"That's quite a story, Lieutenant. Now, what do we learn from all this?"

"Don't necessarily let someone off the hook because they have an alibi, and don't necessarily suspect someone because they haven't or because they refuse to explain themselves. And . . ."

"And what?" she asked quickly.

"And don't necessarily follow the above rules, either. That clear enough?"

They both broke into laughter, the horror of Myra Wahl's death temporarily forgotten.

"So after all this," she said, "what do your instincts tell you about Daniel Winter?"

"Are you asking personally or professionally?" Cerezzi smiled.

Brenda slapped her right hand on his desk. "You're impossible, damn you. Oh, all right. My interest is personal— not professional. Are you happy?"

"I'm a cautious guy, Brenda," he said, more seriously. "And until we catch the murderer I'm not letting your friend the rabbi off the hook. But offhand, I think you're safe with him. On the other hand, I don't know if you should go falling in love with the guy."

She flushed. "Oh? And why not?"

"Because my instinct tells me he spent Sunday night with another woman. Is that reason good enough for you?"

Glumly, Brenda nodded.

The phone rang. Cerezzi answered and then handed the receiver to Brenda, leaning back in his chair to sip his coffee.

"Yes, that's me," he heard her say. "That's right. I'm a psychologist, not a police officer." Her eyes widened. "Can you come over right now? . . . Half an hour. . . . Fine, I can do that. . . . Your name? . . . Well, second name too. . . . Good. . . . Okay. Thank you. See you soon."

The lieutenant looked at her expectantly.

"You heard about Daniel's announcement on the radio yesterday?"

"Yeah, thanks to him we've been flooded with crank calls for two days."

"Well this woman," and Brenda pointed to the phone excitedly, "heard someone threaten Myra Wahl on Sunday afternoon. Before the radio show."

The lieutenant let out a low whistle.

"Did she sound normal?"

"Upset. But I think she's legitimate."

"When she gets here, ring me. I want to be in with you on the questioning."

"I'm sorry, Lieutenant. She said she would speak to me as a psychologist. No police officers present."

"For Pete's sake, Brenda, we're talking about first degree murder."

"I know, Lieutenant." She flashed him a determined look.

"Okay, okay. Just tell me her name."

"Janet Karp."

Cerezzi shuffled papers again. And then whistled.

"What's that supposed to mean, Lieutenant?"

"That you're not meeting with Janet Karp alone."

"But Lieutenant—"

"No buts, Brenda. I warned you about my instincts. My seventh sense tells me that this upset lady is going to bust this case wide open."

Wednesday Afternoon

"Pico Boulevard Temple. Good afternoon," the reception-ist answered the phone.

"This is Reverend Joanne Short of the University of the Southlands. I was a friend of Rabbi Wahl. I'd like to speak to her secretary, please."

"That would be Debbie Berkowitz, Reverend."

Seconds later, Joanne Short started to introduce herself again. Debbie Berkowitz cut in. "Of course I know who you are, Reverend. Rabbi Wahl was a big fan of yours. She used to say that if the two of you ever got any power, all the problems of women, Judaism, and Christianity would be solved in a few hours." Debbie Berkowitz started to laugh, but suddenly she gulped hard. "Excuse me, Reverend, I just can't believe she's dead."

"Me too," Joanne Short said, touched by the genuineness of the woman's emotions. "Please call me Joanne. And I'll call you Debbie, okay?"

"Of course."

"Ever since Myra was killed," Joanne Short went on, "I've been absolutely obsessed. I've gone over her death, again and again, trying to figure out who did it. And then suddenly this morning I thought of something entirely new. It's a hunch and I couldn't think of any way of checking it out, until it dawned on me that you might be able to help me."

"Me, Reverend? How can I . . . ?"

"Listen, Debbie, I need to ask you some things. Is that okay with you?"

"Sure. I'll do whatever I can."

96

"Good. Could you come to my house after work, say about five-thirty?"

"Yes."

Joanne Short gave her the address and directions.

"Is this going to be dangerous? Because maybe we should go to the police."

"Don't worry, Debbie. I just think you might have the answer to a question that's been puzzling me. And if that answer adds up to anything, don't worry—I'm going straight to the cops."

"Okay, Reverend—"

"Joanne," she corrected.

"Okay, Joanne. I'll be there."

The young woman squirmed uncomfortably in her chair, her thin body taut. She seemed hardly more than twenty. Her normally pretty face was drawn and pale, and her large brown eyes had dark shadows under them. She grimaced at Cerezzi, then turned to Brenda.

"You're a psychologist, aren't you? I was sure I'd be able to meet with you alone."

"I don't want to mislead you, Ms. Karp. I am a psychologist, but my employer is the LA police department. Which means that I'm not here to do private counseling. My job is to help this department solve murders. That's why Lieutenant Cerezzi is here with us now."

"I don't know if I want to talk with you, then." Janet Karp started to rise from her seat.

"Wait a minute," Cerezzi instructed grimly. "You're not going anywhere just yet."

"Why not?" Bravely said, but her voice trembled. "I haven't done anything."

"Yes, you have." Cerezzi had been a cop long enough to recognize terror when he saw it. This girl, he decided, would not be hard to break. "Less than an hour ago, you told Dr. Goldstein that you heard someone threaten Myra Wahl the day she was murdered. That makes you a material witness, and the DA can compel you to testify. And if you're thinking of not telling us what you heard, we just might charge you as an accessory after the fact, *to murder*."

Janet Karp collapsed back into her seat, her face was ashen.

Brenda Goldstein looked reassuringly at Janet. "I'm sure, Lieutenant, that Ms. Karp has every intention of cooperating. She wouldn't be here otherwise. I think, though, your presence here is making her very uncomfortable. So why don't you leave the two of us alone?"

"I'll be back soon," Cerezzi barked, and walked out. Once outside, his face broke into a wide grin. Brenda Goldstein was all right, he thought.

Inside, the girl was visibly trembling.

"Is that true what he said, Dr. Goldstein, that they can make me testify against my will?"

Brenda nodded.

"Can they make me testify against *anybody*?" she asked in a small voice.

"Anyone except your husband. Are you married?"

The girl shook her head.

"Can they make me testify against my father?"

"Was it your father who threatened Myra Wahl?"

Mutely, the girl nodded.

"When?"

"About noon on Sunday." Briefly Janet told Brenda of her estrangement from her father, how she had come home that morning to make peace, and how she had gone down to the synagogue to meet him. And then, haltingly, she told of the quarrel she had overheard and of Milton Karp's parting words: 'Watch your step, little girl, I think you ought to leave this job now, while you're still in good health.'"

"When I heard him say that, I ran. I felt absolutely terrible. After all, it was because of me that my father hated Myra, and now it looked like she was going to destroy him with information that I—fool that I was—had given her. I couldn't bear to look at either of them. Later on, I calmed down a bit. I knew that if I could only *speak* to Myra, I could get her to back down, maybe even call my father and take back her threat.

Then I'd have been able to work something out with him. At least so that Myra could finish her contract."

"Did you speak with Myra on Sunday?"

"No. I was too upset. I decided to call her the next day at the temple."

"What about your father? Did you see him on Sunday?"

"No. To tell you the truth, I was afraid to see him. You see, he now knew that I had told Myra about his past. He would have killed me," and then she stopped, horrified at the new meaning the cliché had suddenly assumed. "I checked into a motel and stayed there the rest of the day. Monday morning I called the temple to speak to Myra, and that's how I found out what happened. I was very upset, of course—Myra was my friend—but it never entered my mind that my father might be involved. Then yesterday afternoon I was in my car, listening to Daniel Winter on the radio. And I heard him say that the police think Myra's death was no accident. I began to shake so hard I had to pull over to the side of the road. I thought I was going to be sick. At the end of the show, I scribbled down the phone numbers he'd said to call. But I didn't do anything, I couldn't. I was paralyzed. I didn't sleep at all last night. And then this morning I read in the *Times* that the police are convinced that Myra's death was murder. I couldn't hold it in any longer. I had to tell somebody. I remembered what Winter had said, that you were a psychologist. I thought I could speak with you first, without having to talk to the police."

Brenda nodded sympathetically. "Look, obviously I'm going to have to give all this information to Lieutenant Cerezzi. And he's going to have to look into your father's whereabouts on Sunday evening. But Janet, there's a good chance that this is all a horrible coincidence."

Janet Karp attempted a wan smile. It faded a moment later when Cerezzi knocked and came back into the room. Brenda reviewed what Janet had told him. When Brenda finished, he turned to the young woman and spoke gently, moving into the chair beside her with a grace unusual in a man of his size.

"I know this is very stressful for you, Ms. Karp. But I'm going to have to ask you a few more questions."

The girl nodded. Her face was still very pale, but her features were more composed.

"What is your parent's address?"

"12466 Esther Avenue."

Brenda frowned.

"And who are their next-door neighbors?"

The girl looked at him, puzzled, then shrugged: "Oscar and Dorothy Kramer on one side and Orrin and Maggie Lewis on the other."

Brenda Goldstein's face tensed. Janet Karp shot her a frightened glance.

"Do you know the Lewises?" Cerezzi was impassive.

"Uh-huh," she said uneasily, mesmerized by his toneless interrogation.

"Are they good friends with your parents?"

"So-so. Well, actually I suppose you could say they were. There's one favor my father always does for Orrin Lewis."

"Oh, and what's that?"

"The Lewises travel a lot, and when they're gone my father takes care of their car."

"What do you mean, takes care of their car?"

"Is there a reason why you're asking this, Lieutenant?"

He nodded, fingering his smooth chin, his eyes fixed on her face.

"Well, he leaves my father the key, and my father starts it up every few days, makes sure the battery's okay, things . . ."

She intercepted the electric look that passed between Brenda Goldstein and Joe Cercezzi and stopped, then turned wordlessly toward Cerezzi. Fear was naked in her eyes.

"What should I know that you're not telling me, Lieutenant?"

Cerezzi said nothing. Brenda walked over and put her hand over the girl's.

"There's no reason not to tell her, Lieutenant, is there?"

"I suppose not. . . . Ms. Karp, I'm afraid I have some bad news for you. I'm afraid we're going to have bring your father in for questioning."

"Why?"

"Because the automobile that struck and killed Myra Wahl belonged to Orrin Lewis."

Joanne Short escorted Debbie Berkowitz to the door and stood on the porch with her, shading her eyes against the sun. "Thank you so much for coming."

The girl looked at her quizzically. "Are you sure that's all you wanted to ask me?"

"Yes."

"Tell me, did I help you at all?"

"Yes."

"You're driving me crazy, Joanne. What's the story—is your hunch right or wrong?"

"I don't know yet. I have to do some more checking."

"But Joanne, I—"

"Now don't you worry," Joanne Short cut into her protest, putting an arm around the girl's shoulders. "I'll keep you posted. By the way, let me have your home phone."

The girl pulled a sheet out of her purse and jotted it down. "But I'll be out of town until Saturday night. You see, since Myra was killed, I've been under an awful strain. So Rabbi Rappaport said I could take a few days off. Besides," she added gloomily, "there's not much for me to do at the temple right now."

"Where are you heading?"

"My boyfriend and I are just getting into the car and going South. Mexico, probably. I'll call you Saturday as soon as I get back."

"Do that." Joanne Short smiled.

Debbie Berkowitz started down the narrow brick steps. Suddenly she swung round. "Do me a favor, Joanne. Go to the police."

Joanne Short shrugged.

"When the time's right, I will. Don't you worry."

She watched the girl get into her car and drive away. Then she went back into her house. She'd do a little more checking, sure. But that would just be frosting on the cake. Because Debbie Berkowitz had confirmed it. This was no hunch.

Wednesday Night

Two patrolman pulled up to 12466 Esther Avenue promptly at seven P.M. Ruth Karp opened the door.

"Hello, ma'am. Are you Mrs. Karp?"

She nodded mutely, her eyes on their uniforms.

"Is Mr. Milton . . ." the taller patrolman started, but before he could finish, Milton Karp joined his wife at the door.

"I'm Milton Karp," he said. His manner was hearty and self-assured—in striking contrast to his wife's.

"Excuse me, sir. We have a warrant here to bring you downtown for questioning in relation to the murder of Myra Wahl. Could you please come with us right now?"

Ruth Karp looked from one to the other, her fingers clenching the doorknob, the knuckles white. Milton put a hand on her shoulder. "They probably want to ask some more questions about Orrin's car. Why don't you just put my dinner in the fridge, and we'll heat it up when I get back home?"

"I'm sorry, sir," said the taller policeman, embarrassed. "I think you'd better take along a toothbrush and some pajamas."

As the two men escorted Milton Karp to the patrol car, the taller one glanced back. Ruth Karp was standing frozen in the doorway.

Wednesday night already, Daniel thought, and I haven't started on Saturday's sermon. Not good. He picked up the synagogue bulletin and turned to the calendar section. "Saturday, February 9, the rabbi will speak on 'Between Parents and Children: The Fifth Commandment Revisited.'" That is, he thought sourly, if I prepare something. He took the last can of

102

soda out of the refrigerator and popped open the tab. Then he went into his study. His eyes scanned the variety of Bibles in his bookcase. Orthodox, Conservative, Reform, Protestant, and Catholic commentaries all lay there—in an ecumenicism, he thought, possible only on shelves. He settled finally on a volume of Exodus. It was a classic Jewish edition, all in Hebrew, with the Bible text surrounded by ten medieval commentaries. He sat down in his reclining chair and eased backward. Already he had an idea of the direction he wanted to take. The Bible instructs us to love God. And neighbors. And strangers. But not our parents. Why? He started reading the commentaries.

He was deeply immersed when the doorbell shattered his concentration. Automatically, he looked at his watch. After ten. Feeling unaccountably anxious, he moved toward the door, the book still in his hand. The bell shrilled again. As if that were not enough, this was followed by forceful knocking. Daniel looked through the peephole. Wilbur Kantor stood there, without an overcoat, panting. Daniel opened the door.

"I have some terrible news." The heavily-built man charged in, all amenities ignored. "Milt Karp has been arrested for the murder of Myra Wahl."

Daniel thought back to the bald man with the curved nose who had spoken at the funeral.

"It sounds like one of those crazy rumors, Wilbur. You didn't hear it on the radio, did you?"

Wilbur Kantor collapsed heavily on the couch and waited until his breathing returned to normal.

"No, Rabbi. From his wife."

Daniel was speechless. He felt a mixture of emotions, most of them sad. For Karp's family. For Myra. And for the Jewish community. This is just the sort of scandal we don't need, he thought. He sat down next to Kantor.

"Can you tell me what Mrs. Karp told you?"

"That's why I came here, Rabbi," Kantor said, adjusting his glasses with hands that were far from steady. "Ruth Karp insisted I speak to you. You see, Milt and I are golf buddies. We've played every Tuesday afternoon now for I don't know how many—probably twelve, fifteen years. Anyway, Ruth told me the police came to their house this evening and took Milt off for some questioning—"

"Questioning? Or did they arrest him?"

"Well, they didn't exactly arrest him then. But they told him to take pajamas, stuff like that, with him. Ruth immediately called up Hank Weisgal, their lawyer, and he told her to sit tight, that he'd go down and see if he could do anything, but that it didn't sound like they were planning to release Milt real soon. Ruth, as you can imagine, was nervous enough as it was. And now, Rabbi, comes the unbelievable part. About an hour ago, Ruth got a call from Janet—that's their daughter. Between you and me, Rabbi, Janet's a bit of a nut. Hasn't even been on speaking terms with Milt for a year or so. Blames him for all her problems. You know, all that Freudian crap. Milt talked to me about it once. He even had a notion that Wahl was somehow behind the kid's behavior. . . ."

"Wilbur," Daniel broke in, "tell me what happened an hour ago."

"That's what I'm trying to tell you," the older man snapped, annoyed at the interruption. "An hour ago, Janet called up her mother, hysterical, to tell her that she had heard Milt threatening Wahl on Sunday morning and that she had gone to the police with that information."

"Wait. This is important, Wilbur. Did Janet tell Ruth why he was threatening Myra?"

"I gather, and I'm guessing here, Rabbi, because Ruth was very vague, that Wahl knew something about Milt—I don't know, I assume something pretty embarrassing."

"Myra Wahl was *blackmailing* him?"

"Listen, Rabbi, I don't know. I do know from some of the other guys at the temple that they were angling to fire her, and I suppose she got wind of it and threatened Milt."

"Wait a second, Wilbur; I'm getting mixed up. Just who threatened who?"

"Well, like I said, Wahl threatened to expose some scandal about Milt, and apparently Janet heard her father threaten Wahl. You know, one of those things you say when you're all heated up, like watch out for your health, or something."

"And Karp's daughter told this to the police?"

"Wait, Rabbi, it gets worse. It turns out that the car that killed Myra Wahl belongs to the Karp's next-door neighbor."

"Oh, my God."

"It's worse than that, Rabbi. You see, the neighbors were away, and Milt had duplicates of their car keys."

Unable to sit still, Daniel paced about the room, digesting all this information. Suddenly he turned to Wilbur, his eyes narrowed. "Why exactly are you telling me all this, Wilbur?"

"Well, you see, Rabbi," he said carefully, "I don't mean no offense, but indirectly you're responsible for this whole mess."

"What exactly does that mean?"

"On your radio program yesterday, you urged people to call up the cops if they had any information." Wilbur waited for Daniel's acknowledging nod, then continued, "Well, somehow Janet heard about it, and that's what put it into her head to go to some psychologist you mentioned."

"Brenda Goldstein."

"Yeah, something like that. Well, this Goldstein took whatever Janet Karp told her straight to the cops."

"I'm not surprised, Wilbur," Daniel said heatedly. "I did announce on the air, you know, that Brenda Goldstein is a police psychologist. Now, tell me, why did Ruth Karp ask you to speak with me?"

"She's frantic, Rabbi. She doesn't know who to turn to. All Hank Weisgal can say is wait. Anyway, she's got it into her head that because of that announcement you made you must have some kind of in with these people. Do you?"

"I know the police psychologist," Daniel said noncommittally. "As a matter of fact, she's a member of our congregation."

"Wonderful. That's great, Rabbi. Well, then, call her up. Say you gotta speak with her."

"Wilbur, what do you expect me to say? I'm very sad for Ruth Karp, but even from the little you're telling me the evidence sounds damning."

"Rabbi, you gotta do something to at least make sure the police keep on looking for someone else. Listen to me. I've known Milt Karp ages. I don't care what the evidence is, I *know* he didn't do it. You've got to tell that to the police."

"Wilbur, I'm a rabbi, not a magician."

Wilbur Kantor frowned at Daniel, his eyes level under

drawn brows. "Rabbi, you and I have not been the closest of friends, have we?"

"I suppose not."

"And I've never asked you for a favor before—that is, a personal favor for me, not for the synagogue—have I?"

"No, you haven't," Daniel conceded. He knew what was coming.

"Well, I'm asking you now, Rabbi. Ruth Karp called me up. You are the only person she knows of with any connections in the police department. She called me because I was the only one she knows who can get to you. What are you telling me to do, Rabbi? Call that poor woman and tell her you turned me down flat?"

Daniel put a hand on his forehead and let out a long sigh.

"If I'm going to do anything at all, I'm going to need to speak to Milton Karp first. Can his wife make sure he'll agree to see me?"

"I'm sure that can be worked out."

"And I'll speak to whomever I can at the police and pressure them not to close off their investigation. But I'm not promising anything. Okay?"

"Bless you, Rabbi. I'll call Ruth right now and tell her. I feel a lot better already."

Daniel wished he could say the same.

He tried Brenda's house twice and then phoned her office. Dr. Goldstein was still in, a clipped voice said, but not available. He left an urgent message. A half hour later he tried again. "Rabbi," the exasperated clerk told him, "I wasn't giving you a line. Dr. Goldstein cannot be disturbed now. I promise you, she'll get your message as soon as she's free."

Unable to concentrate, Daniel paced his living room. What little Kantor had told him sounded very bad. And yet—and yet—the evidence was so damning, so perfect, that he couldn't help but feel something was not quite right. He thought back to his old Talmud rebbe, Elyakim Schwartz, who had taught him Tractate Sanhedrin on Jewish criminal law. Rabbi Schwartz had a favorite law in it. "In America, you know, boys, to convict somebody you need a unanimous jury. What do they say here, if one jury member says innocent then the jury is hung instead of the defendant? But we Jews are different. According to the Talmud, if the jury is unanimous, that's just when we don't convict. It means something is fishy. It means that everyone was so sure of the man's guilt that nobody tried to put up a vigorous defense." Schwartz went on to explain that in Jewish courts there was no prosecutor or defense attorney. "Nobody to make his living getting people off, even when he knows they are guilty." The twenty-three judges, who also made up the jury, appointed members among themselves to try to find mitigating evidence on behalf of the defendant. "And if no one was willing to do it, if not a single one of the twenty-three could find something good to say about the defendant, then they didn't convict. We Jews don't want to have, what do they say here . . . a kangaroo court." At the time, Daniel remembered that he thought the law foolish. "What about Jack Ruby?" he had demanded. "Millions of people, including most of us here, saw him shoot Lee Harvey Oswald on live television. Are you saying that we should question that fact just because we all agree on it?" Schwartz had an answer, but it hadn't satisfied Daniel. Strange, then, how Schwartz's words came back to him now, clear as a bell. No kangaroo court. If everyone agrees, something is fishy. He kept pacing. The case against Karp seemed so pat. And yet a few things jarred. He drifted out of his living room, into the kitchen. He was heavily into a salami and coleslaw sandwich when the phone rang. It was Brenda.

"Daniel," she said excitedly, "it's not too late, is it?"

"No," he said, "I'm too wound up to sleep."

"You're not going to believe why I'm calling."

"Because you think you caught Myra's killer and his name is Milton Karp."

There was silence at the end of the line. "How in heaven's name did you know?" she stammered. "We haven't released that information yet—not to the press, not to anyone."

He filled her in on Wilbur Kantor's visit, including Ruth Karp's request that he intercede.

"I'm afraid you're wasting your time, Daniel. I was in with Cerezzi during the questioning. After he was formally charged, Karp clammed up, but honestly, Daniel, I don't think there's a snowball's chance in hell that he's innocent."

"And yet . . ."

"And yet what?"

"Many things. But I need to speak with Karp. Will Cerezzi allow it?"

"If Karp's lawyer doesn't object, I expect it will be okay."

"Good."

"You're a hard one to figure out, Daniel Winter. I thought you'd be pleased when I told you the news."

He tried to make light of her petulant tone.

"Happy? To find out that the president of a synagogue murdered the rabbi? It hardly gives me a sense of security."

"I'm serious, Daniel. I felt good tonight. We caught the killer. The lieutenant's going to stop hounding you. I thought we'd go out and celebrate."

"We will, Brenda," he promised warmly. "Let's just make sure first that Karp's guilty."

They hung up. Daniel got into bed, but he couldn't sleep. He tossed restlessly and finally turned on the light and tried to concentrate on a novel. When that didn't work, he flipped on the television. When the phone rang again, after one, it was a welcome respite.

"This is Hank Weisgal," the deep voice drawled. "I'm sorry to be calling at this hour, but Ruth Karp insisted." Weisgal sketched in the events of the evening, but added little to what Kantor had already told Daniel. "Anyway, Rabbi, personally I don't see how you can do any good, but Ruth insists that you speak to Milton."

"I'll do it," he answered. The lawyer's skepticism left a sour feeling in the pit of his stomach.

"Listen, Rabbi. Are you really tight with Cerezzi and that shrink?"

"I think they have some regard for me."

"Well, I hope they do. Things don't look good."

"When should I come down?" Daniel asked. Weisgal was depressing him. He just wanted to end the conversation and go to sleep.

"Be there about nine-thirty tomorrow morning," the lawyer said. "Okay?"

"Fine," Daniel said, and hung up.

Thursday Morning

Joanne Short untied the twist sealing the plastic garbage bag. She plunged her hand in and pulled out a slightly soggy *Los Angeles Times*. She checked the date—Wednesday, February 6—and threw the paper aside. Sighing, she began systematically to examine the bag's contents. She delved through some old copies of *Ms.* magazine. Gingerly, she put her hand in deeper, to the bottom. No more *Times*. Dammit. She retied the bag and set off in her car.

She stopped in front of the Pico-Doheny Newsstand and ran over to the outdoor racks. High stacks of that day's *Times* confronted her. Near the bottom, one paper looked slightly yellowed. She bent down and started tugging it loose.

"Stop messing up my papers, lady," a voice bawled. A man in his fifties, with a bulging chin, wearing a checkered flannel shirt, emerged belligerently from the newsstand. "Whatsa matter with you? They're all the same."

"I thought you might have older papers on the bottom."

He looked at her as if she were mad.

"I'm looking for the Monday *Times*," she said.

"Why didn't you say so? Lemme check inside."

She followed him. His head disappeared under the front counter and a moment later bobbed up. "Not exactly mint condition," he said, smoothing out a front-page rip.

She paid him, took the paper back to her car, and impatiently started flipping pages. It took only seconds to find the article she wanted. She read it twice and then carefully tore it out, folded it up, and tucked it into her purse. Her lips were pulled into a grim, determined line. Just one more step.

* * *

Milton Karp stood up, one hand on the scuffed metal chair beside him. He held up the worn Bible that prison officials had provided him at his request.

"I didn't kill Myra Wahl, Rabbi. I swear it."

Daniel said nothing. It was hard to believe that this desperate man standing opposite him was the same person he had heard solemnly eulogize Myra Wahl forty-eight hours earlier. One thing was clear. Since last night, Milton Karp's entire world had collapsed.

"You don't believe me, Rabbi, do you?"

"I don't believe you, I don't not believe you," Daniel began, choosing his words carefully. The tension lifted ever so slightly from Karp's tight face, where the worry lines now seemed indelibly engraved. "On the other hand, the issue isn't what *I* believe, it's the evidence."

"But it's all circumstantial—"

"Which is why my mind is still open," Daniel interrupted. "But as things stand now, Mr. Karp, you're guilty until you can prove otherwise. You realize that, don't you?"

"What sort of stupid question is that?" Karp yelled, his features contorted. Then the fight seemed to go out of him, and he slumped back into the chair. His shoulders sagged in defeat. "Excuse me, Rabbi. Of course I realize the spot I'm in. The truth of the matter is, it doesn't make any difference if you or Weisgal, for that matter, believe I'm innocent. No one can help me."

"Then why did you agree to see me?"

"Because you're a rabbi." He smiled faintly at Daniel's baffled look. "I need to speak to a rabbi."

"But Reuben Rappaport is your rabbi?"

"Reuben means well, but he's a fool."

Daniel chose to ignore the comment. "Why me?"

"Wilbur tells me that you're ambitious and stubborn and that you think a lot of yourself." Daniel grinned, reluctantly. "But he also says you're bright. That's what I need now, a rabbi with brains."

"To do what?"

Karp leaned his head back against the wall behind him.

He did not take his eyes off the rabbi. He stroked his chin pensively, and several minutes passed before he spoke.

"You probably think I'm full of crap when I tell you I'm a religious man. But I am. Sure, I'll go into a restaurant and order a lobster thermidor without thinking twice. For all I know that makes me a goy in your eyes. But right here where it counts," and Karp thumped against his heart, "I know there's a God. And that's why I need a rabbi. I want to do the right thing. But I swear I don't know what the right thing is at this minute. Do you understand what I'm saying?"

"The words, yes," Daniel said, frowning.

"I didn't sleep a wink last night. I kept going over and over this nightmare." Now that he had begun, the words spilled out. "Rabbi, I'm being framed, and there's nothing I can do about it."

"Do you know who's framing you?"

Karp nodded miserably.

"Then what are you waiting for? Tell the police."

"I can't."

"Oh, and why not?" Daniel said coldly. He was beginning to understand why the police found his own meddling so amusing.

"You know why I can't go to the cops?" Karp exploded. His eyes roamed anxiously around the drab conference room, and then he disciplined his voice. "Because it's my own daughter who's framing me." The man put his head down in his hands and began to sob brokenly. At a loss, Daniel waited. "You're a rabbi, you tell me what I'm supposed to do," Karp whispered hoarsely.

"I can't answer that, Mr. Karp. Did you really think I could? Do you want to tell me what makes you think your daughter's framing you?"

The man controlled himself with difficulty. "When you think it through, it's pretty obvious. Who else, other than my wife and Janet, knew I had the keys to the Lewises' car? And who else knew I had a fight that day with Wahl? And in case the cops didn't connect me to the car, who showed up to tell them about that fight?"

"You think your *daughter* murdered Myra Wahl?"

Karp nodded stiffly. "I can't think of any other explanation."

"What possible motive could she have?"

"To destroy me. Do you know that she hasn't spoken to me in a year, ever since she moved out of our house? What do you think of that?"

"Plenty of children have disagreements with their fathers without murdering people and framing them."

"So what are you saying, Rabbi, that I'm guilty? And tell me, did you ever hear of a parent murdering someone and setting up his own child?"

"Mr. Karp, I've already told you I don't know if you're guilty or not. But I'm here because I want to know. Now, may I ask you a few questions?"

Karp nodded.

"From what I understand, your daughter told Lieutenant Cerezzi that she overheard you threaten Myra Wahl. Did you?"

"Yes, I did. But do you also know what the provocation was?"

"I heard something, but I don't know if it's true. Why don't we start from the beginning?"

"Okay, but everything I'm telling you now must be in confidence. Okay?"

"Yes."

"It's hard for me to talk about this, I've spent so many years hiding it. When I was twenty-seven, Rabbi—and mind you I'm fifty-nine now—I was an accountant for a clothing manufacturer in Chicago. It was my first job and I felt very lucky. The company was growing about fifty percent a year, and there I was a *pisher* in my twenties, their accountant. Anyway the company went public, over the counter. The stock was hot—it came out in August at ten and by November was selling at over thirty. Then that Christmas season they laid a bomb. Two or three big items just didn't move at all. When it came time to issue the earnings, the chairman of the board and the president—the guys who had given me the job—came to me with a sheet and told me to sign it. It was a false earnings report. They said that if I didn't certify it, the stock would fall to nothing and hundreds of people, including me, would be out of work. So I signed it. Later I found out that they sold their stock before the real news came out and made a killing. It didn't do them much good. We all got caught. I spent two and half years in prison. I got out, took my mother's maiden name, and left Chicago. I'm no saint, Rabbi, but since the day I left that prison I haven't cheated anyone out of a penny." Karp hesitated, trying to read Daniel's expression. "No one in LA aside from Ruth and Janet knows about it. You can imagine how people would've reacted to me," he said bitterly, "if they'd known I was an ex-con. I wouldn't have had a chance. Anyway, I'm just giving you the background, so you'll understand my fight with Myra Wahl. You see, on Sunday morning the executive comittee demanded Wahl's resignation."

"Why?"

"She was a problem, Rabbi. Look, the lady's dead now and I don't want to say anything bad about her. But when I tell you she was very difficult to get along with, I think you understand what I mean." There was a shadow of a smile in his exhausted eyes. "From what I hear, you had your own problems with her."

"Go on," Daniel said, refusing to comment.

"Anyway, it wasn't just me who wanted her out. We went around the room and it was unanimous. After the meeting, Wahl came up to speak to me. The others had left. She blamed the whole thing on me."

"Was there any truth in that?"

Karp shook his head.

"But didn't you blame her for turning your daughter against you?"

Karp shifted in his seat. "Listen, I had no love for the lady. But for that matter, neither did anybody else. Sure, I spoke to some of the guys. But I promise you, I didn't have to twist a single arm to get them to agree."

"Okay. So what happened when Wahl confronted you?"

"She started acting crazy, Rabbi, making threats, saying that Janet had told her I'd been in prison and that if we fired her she'd make sure that became public knowledge."

"And that, I gather, is when you threatened her?"

"A threat?" Karp shrugged. "I suppose you could call it that. But it was nothing specific. I said something like, watch your step, or your health, one of those dumb things you hear people say in movies all the time. But it didn't mean anything." He looked at Daniel defensively. "What do you think I was planning to do?"

"I don't know, Mr. Karp. You were the one who made the remark."

"Only because I was scared, Rabbi. And I wanted to scare her. That's all there was to it."

"Did you know Janet had overheard you?"

"No. I only found that out later. You see when I left Myra I saw a woman running away, and I realized she must have heard what we'd said. I chased after her but I couldn't catch up. Then when I got home, Ruth told me Janet had gone down to the temple to see me." His face brightened for a moment. "Forget proof, Rabbi. Logically speaking, does it make sense to you that I would threaten someone, find out I had been overheard, and still go ahead and kill them? Wouldn't that be a pretty stupid thing to do?"

"It would be stupid," Daniel agreed. "Unfortunately for you, the police will probably say that you're not the first stupid murderer." Karp tapped his right foot nervously on the floor. "But tell me, do you think Myra really would have blackmailed you?"

"When she said it I was sure she meant to do it. But later on we came—that is, I'm sure we would have come to some understanding."

"What does that mean," Daniel exclaimed, "you *came* to an understanding?"

"I didn't say that, Rabbi. I said we would have come to an understanding."

"That's not what you said the first time." Daniel insisted. "Mr. Karp, after you left the temple that afternoon did you see Myra Wahl again?"

"When could I have?"

"Just answer my question, please."

"No."

"Are you sure?"

"What are you getting at, Rabbi?"

A prison guard came over, forcing them to lower their voices. "Five minutes more." Daniel waited, burning with impatience, till the man moved away.

"Ever since I found out about Myra Wahl's death, something's puzzled me. Myra was a good runner. She'd run to the studio in about forty minutes. Yet she was killed over an hour after she left the station, and she wasn't even halfway home. To me that suggests that she stopped along the way to meet someone. It wasn't you, Mr. Karp, was it?"

Karp chewed on his lip. "Why would I do something like that?"

"Because you intended to come to an understanding with her. Are you sure you didn't?"

Karp watched Daniel, silently.

"According to your story," Daniel hurried on, "when Myra Wahl threatened you, you panicked. Now you tell me you *assumed* that you'd come to an understanding with her. Either you're lying to me, and the reason you stopped panicking is because you killed Myra Wahl. Or you didn't kill her, and you stopped panicking because the two of you came to an understanding. I'm asking you again, Mr. Karp, did you drive over to KLAX, follow Myra Wahl, and speak with her?"

"And if I did, Rabbi, do you think it would help me to tell the cops? The way I figure it, if I admit to a midnight meeting with Wahl, I'm buying a one-way ticket to a life sentence."

Daniel exhaled slowly and decided to change tactics.

"Right now, according to you, there are two alternatives. Either you killed Myra Wahl or your daughter did and framed you. As far as you're concerned, both scenarios are singularly horrific. So tell me, please, what precisely do you want me to do for you?"

Karp swallowed hard. "I want you to speak with Janet. And . . . and . . . I want you to tell her that what's done is done. She can't take back what she said. I understand that. And tell her," his head was bowed low, "that she's safe, I've hurt her enough. I won't do anything more to hurt her. Tell her I forgive her, and I'm not going to tell the cops a thing. Can you do that for me, Rabbi? I'd do it myself, but I don't think there's any way they will let me see her."

"I'll do it, Mr. Karp. But there's something I want you to do for me."

"What's that?"

"I'm giving you some advice and I want you to follow it. But only if you're innocent."

"I am innocent, Rabbi."

"Then tell the police that you met with Myra Wahl Sunday night."

Karp's eyes met Daniel's with a fierce defiance. "I never said that I met her."

"You'd better tell them. Because they're going to find out. And when they do . . ." Daniel dramatically drew his hand across his throat and left the sentence unfinished.

"So suppose I did meet Myra?" Karp challenged. "What good does that do me?"

"A lot." Out of the corner of his eye Daniel saw the guard returning. Their five minutes were up. He leaned forward earnestly. "For one, it suggests to me a third possibility. And it might suggest that to the police as well."

"I don't follow you."

Daniel looked quickly at the guard. The man tapped impatiently at his watch. Daniel held up one finger, pleading for a little more time. He turned to Karp.

"Listen to me. If you're innocent, your only hope now is to tell the truth."

Karp's glance flickered to the guard. He spoke in a whisper.

"I'm not interested in the truth, Rabbi. Because the truth will convict my daughter as a murderess. Don't you understand that?"

"Tell me something, Mr. Karp. Do you love your daughter?"

"Would I be doing this if I didn't?" It was an anguished cry, and Daniel steeled himself to be firm.

"I'll tell you what I think. Maybe you do love Janet. In your own way. But you don't trust her one iota. You call it love to suspect your daughter's a murderer? That's ridiculous. To hell with loving your daughter. Maybe you'd do better to trust her a little. *That's why you've got to tell the truth.*"

Karp looked down at his shoes. "I'll think about what you said, Rabbi. I really will. And you, will you go speak to Janet?"

Daniel nodded and stood up.

"Wilbur Kantor was right." Karp said suddenly.

"About what?"

"He told me once that you were a pain in the ass, but smart. I agree with him. Most rabbis I've known have been pains in the ass and stupid."

"Thanks for the compliment." The corners of Daniel's mouth lifted ever so slightly. "Someday I'll tell you what we rabbis say about synagogue presidents."

It took Daniel ten minutes of reckless driving to get from the downtown prison to the fortress-like edifice that housed homicide headquarters. He headed straight for Brenda's office, almost knocking over a clerk in the corridor.

"Ah, Rabbi Perry Mason!" she greeted him with mock ceremony as he entered. "Still insist your client's innocent?"

"He's not my client, Brenda, and I didn't say he was innocent," Daniel spoke sternly, but then he saw the laughter in her green eyes, and he smiled reluctantly. "Anyway, what are you in such a good mood about?"

"Because we caught a murderer."

"And you're so sure he's guilty?"

"Daniel, we've got the motive, the weapon, the opportunity—and they all spell Milton Karp. Joe says that outside of a confession, this is about as open and shut as they come. In fact, he's taking bets that Karp will confess inside of two days."

Confess? It wouldn't surprise Daniel. At the moment he could imagine the man confessing to anything, if he thought it would save his daughter.

"Oh, come off it, Daniel. Why are you looking so grim? Karp threatens Wahl; then a car—to which he just happens to have the key—runs her down; and his only alibi for the time of the murder is that he was driving around alone." Her brows knit together. "Do you honestly think he might be innocent?"

"Might," he said emphatically, drawing the word out.

"Why?"

"A few things don't make . . ."

The ring of the telephone on her desk stopped him. "Cerezzi," Brenda explained when she hung up after a brief conversation. "Don't go. I'll be back in a minute. I want to hear what you have to say."

Restlessly, he tried to put his thoughts in order. A few things still made no sense to him. Maybe he should set them down on paper. A light tap sounded on the door, and Brenda's secretary came in. "Dr. Goldstein's going to be a little longer than she thought. But she asked that you stay, if possible. All right?"

Daniel nodded, refusing her offer of coffee. He went over to Brenda's desk and searched around for a blank piece of paper. Almost automatically, his eyes were drawn to a pile of neatly stacked folders, the top one labeled Karp, Milton E. He looked inside and found the police account of Karp's conviction in Chicago thirty-two years earlier. Other files lay beneath Karp's. He glanced at their labels, saw one familiar name, and repressing a twinge of conscience, opened it and started reading. That's odd, he thought. Suddenly he heard footsteps, and he quickly slid the file back into place.

Brenda came in, closely followed by Cerezzi.

"Hello, Rabbi," the lieutenant greeted him exuberantly. "Brenda schlepped me here." He barely suppressed a grin. "She tells me you think we're being hasty."

"I'm a novice at these things, Lieutenant; you're the professional. Nevertheless . . ." Daniel chose his words carefully. He wanted, above all, to avoid the tension of their previous encounter.

"Nevertheless what, Rabbi?"

"Let me ask you something, Lieutenant. Does Milton Karp strike you as a stupid man?"

"Not at all."

"Exactly. Yet your entire case against him rests on his being incredibly stupid. If he were going to kill Myra Wahl, why threaten her? For all Karp knew, Myra went off and told a dozen people about his threat. Second—"

"Hold it, Rabbi. Let's take 'em one at a time," Cerezzi interrupted, his voice neutral. "I think the answer to that one is obvious. When Wahl first told Karp she'd expose his past, he blew up. That's a perfectly natural reaction. I don't think his immediate intention was to kill her. He probably decided that later, when he got home. When he'd had time to figure that there was just too much risk she'd expose him."

"That doesn't answer my question. What made Karp so sure Myra hadn't already told people he'd threatened her?"

"Maybe he didn't think about it."

"But that brings me to my second point—how could he not think about it? He knew that Janet had overheard them in the temple corridor, and—"

"Who told you that?"

"Karp did, this morning."

"What did he say to you, Rabbi: 'I knew Janet overheard me, so how could I be so stupid as to have then gone out and killed Wahl'?"

"What the hell!" Daniel exploded, casting aside attempts at conciliation. "*You listened in* on our conversation."

Cerezzi laughed heartily. He was obviously enjoying Daniel's anger. "On the money, wasn't I? No, Rabbi, we don't tap prisoner's conferences. But what else did you expect Karp to tell you? I assure you, *when* he confesses, and he will, he'll admit that he didn't know Janet was there."

"Third," Daniel pressed on, "and this is the grossest stupidity of all—why would Karp use his next-door neighbor's car, to which he has the key, and not expect the police to connect him to the murder?"

"Good question, Rabbi," Cerezzi said absently, picking up an ashtray and then setting it down again. "In retrospect, you're right. Karp looks pretty stupid. But that's only because the daughter told us that he had threatened Wahl. But you want to know something? Before we knew that, I had been out to Karp's house and spoken to him, and it never even occurred to me he might be implicated. If the daughter hadn't come in, there's a good chance we never would have checked into Karp's connection to Wahl."

"Even though he spoke at her funeral?"

"But I wasn't at the funeral, Rabbi. And I doubt that the two cops who were there, or Brenda, remembered the name of the guy giving the eulogy. He took a risk, I'll grant you. But when you consider it, the risk was pretty small."

"Fourth," Daniel resumed stubbornly, although shaken by Cerezzi's easy tone and bemused smile. "Excuse me if I sound like a Jewish chauvinist, Lieutenant, but this is just not the sort of things Jews do."

"If that's what you're left with, Rabbi, I suspect you don't have much of a case. But tell you what, I'll even agree with you on this one—as a rule your people are more law-abiding than most. But there are exceptions, right? You admit that?"

"Of course," Daniel said irritably.

"Brenda, you want to bring the rabbi the file we have on Mr. Karp?" She pulled it off her desk and passed it to Daniel. "Take a look, Rabbi." Daniel made a pretense of carefully reading it, not daring to admit that he had rifled through it earlier.

"So what?" he said, looking up after a few minutes.

"Apparently, your Mr. Karp is one of the exceptions."

"Lieutenant, this is *not* murder." He waved the slim folder with mounting fury. "And in any case, this happened over thirty years ago, Karp hasn't committed a single criminal act since."

"Maybe he just hasn't been caught."

"So much for innocent until proven guilty," Daniel muttered, and then restrained himself. Provoking confrontations wasn't going to help anybody. He forced a smile. "Look, if I sounded like a chauvinist before, maybe I'll sound like an anti-Semite now. You see, what Karp did in Chicago is the sort of crime those Jews who are criminals commit. White-collar, non-violent stuff. But Jews don't murder."

"Really, Rabbi, is that a fact?" Cerezzi asked, bantering him. "Ever hear of Murder Incorporated? It was run like a business, and they murdered hundreds of people. And many of the leaders—plus plenty of the killers, for that matter—were Jews. Meyer Lansky, Lepke Buchalter—whom, if you please, Hoover called 'the most dangerous criminal in the United States'—Mendy Weiss, Bugsy Siegel. Did you ever hear of the Purple Gang in Detroit? Run by Abe Bernstein. They murdered over five hundred people. Want me to go on?"

"I'm not a fool, Lieutenant. I know there have been Jewish killers. But both you and I know that it's rare." Daniel paused, fixed his eyes on Cerezzi, and said firmly. "I stand by what I said. Jews are very unlikely to commit murder."

"And what about Karp's threat to Myra?" Brenda asked.

"The lieutenant himself said it was a *natural reaction* to her threat. Karp was furious and spoke nastily. Just as Myra did. That's a common enough Jewish characteristic—to channel physical violence into verbal aggression."

"What's that supposed to mean?"

"It's a theory of mine," Daniel continued evenly. "As a rule Jews are physically non-aggressive. For example, I've been in Jewish communal life for years, and at meetings I've heard people say the most appalling things to each other, just like Myra did to me on the air. Things that other people would kill for, or at the very least throw a punch. And yet in all that time I've never once seen a fistfight at a Jewish meeting. When Jews get angry, they don't hit, they curse. What's one of the things Yiddish is known for? Curses. Like 'May all your teeth fall out except one and that should ache you.'"

Cerezzi threw back his head and roared with laughter. But when his expression cleared, Daniel saw his words hadn't even made a dent.

"You're a bright man, Rabbi, and I like you. The truth is, I can agree with everything you've said. But it changes nothing. You're making general statements about most Jews and I'm telling you about one individual." He gave Daniel a shrewd glance from under his thick brows. "The news about Karp's arrest will cause a big scandal among the Jewish community here, won't it?"

"Lieutenant," Daniel said, meeting Cerezzi's gaze squarely. "If I thought Karp was guilty, then to hell with the scandal. Look, don't misunderstand me: I'm not claiming he's innocent. I really don't know. All I'm asking you to do is to keep an open mind, keep looking."

"Listen to me carefully, Rabbi. Karp's guilty. All that will happen if we continue investigating is that you Jews will get stuck with an even nastier scandal."

"What does that mean, Lieutenant?" There was a hard edge to Brenda's voice.

"Rabbi Wahl wasn't exactly as pure as the driven snow. You know, Rabbi, the more I looked at the note that was sent to her, the more something in the handwriting didn't look right to me. Neither of you picked up on it, so I didn't say anything. But my instinct was correct. That was definitely a woman's handwriting on the note. In other words, Rabbi Wahl . . . well, I don't have to say it." He looked from Brenda to Daniel. "Did either of you realize that?"

Brenda shook her head, dumbfounded. Daniel made no gesture at all.

"It won't take us long to find the lady. But with Karp charged, I've called off the investigation. You know why? Because Myra Wahl's sexual tastes, however fascinating they might be to the press, have no bearing on her murder. But, Rabbi, if you and others in your community go around telling everyone and his mother that Karp is innocent, and God knows what, poking around, hiring detectives to prove it, you're not going to get Karp off. All you'll end up doing is smearing Myra Wahl and your whole community's name to the high heavens." Daniel waited for him to say *fahrshtein* again, but the lieutenant had apparently finished.

"And what about that phone call to Myra and Joanne Short during the radio show—that means nothing to you?"

"Not in comparison with the solid case we've got against Karp."

Daniel shrugged his shoulders in resignation. "Then I guess I should be going."

"One question before you do. Okay?"

"Okay."

"First," and the lieutenant held out his large hand, "no hard feelings, right?"

Daniel returned his firm grip. "What's your question, Lieutenant?"

"If Karp didn't do it, how the hell did his next-door neighbor's car come to be used as the murder weapon?"

Daniel thought of several answers, but the promise of silence that Karp had exacted kept him mute. Who knows, maybe Janet *was* involved? But more likely, maybe Karp wasn't the only one who followed Myra that evening. Maybe the killer had, too. And seen Karp's meeting with her, and . . . and . . . But he couldn't tell that to Cerezzi, either. It was up to Karp to decide whether or not to admit to his meeting with Myra. And if he didn't—well, Daniel had tried.

"I'm waiting for an answer, Rabbi."

"Let me think about it," Daniel finally offered, weakly.

"You do that. And when you can explain that to me, Rabbi, I'll open up this investigation all over again. Okay?"

Thursday Afternoon

Reverend Joanne Short picked up her phone, punched out the numbers she had scrawled on her notepad, and demanded to speak with Lieutenant Joe Cerezzi.

"The lieutenant's in the building, but he's not here right now," came the polite reply. "Who shall I tell him called?"

"Reverend Joanne Short. And you can also tell him I'm waiting on the line. I'll hold until you locate him."

A full five minutes elapsed before Cerezzi picked up the phone.

"Yes, Reverend," he answered cautiously. The last piece of information Short had given him had proved accurate all right. Nevertheless, the woman's intensity made him uncomfortable.

"I know who the murderer is."

"Well, thank you, Reverend, but so do we. We've just announced the arrest to the press."

"And who are you holding, Lieutenant?"

"Milton Karp."

Silence from the other end, then, "He's not the murderer."

"Really, Reverend. Who is? Do you still think it's Rabbi Winter?"

"I'm not going to play twenty questions with you, Lieutenant. I know who the murderer is, and if you'll hear me out I'll stop you from making an ass of yourself."

Her stubborn certainty was unnerving Cerezzi, despite his conviction that Karp was guilty. This case had far too many clerics in it for his taste. First the rabbi, now the reverend.

"Where are you, Reverend?"

"At home." She gave the address: 10826 Brooke, in West LA.

"I can be there in twenty-five minutes."

"No." She paused. "Come at four o'clock?"

"What's wrong with right now?"

"Lieutenant, right now it's all in my head, but I want to have everything worked out for you on paper."

"Excuse me, Reverend, is this just a pet theory of yours, or do you have hard facts?"

"Be here at four and you'll get all the facts you need."

"Okay," he said. "But let me remind you of one thing. The police department is currently holding a suspect I am morally certain is the murderer. Just remember that, and don't do anything stupid in the meantime."

For a few seconds there was no sound at the other end, but when Joanne Short resumed, her voice could have frozen fire.

"I've figured out who the murderer is, Lieutenant. You and your whole homicide squad haven't. So you tell me who's stupid?"

This time the silence was Cerezzi's.

"You'll be here at four?"

The lieutenant grunted his assent and hung up. Joanne Short stared at the telephone and fleetingly regretted her outburst. But only for a second. There was too much to be done.

She picked up a sheet and reread the script that she had already prepared for her next call. This one's a lot riskier than the one to Cerezzi, she thought. But then again, compared to the possible payoff, the risk seemed small. What choice did she have? The evidence she had for Cerezzi was, she knew, only circumstantial. It might shake his conviction that the man he had under arrest was guilty. But was it enough? This call could make it enough. Her message could force the murderer to flee. And flight in California, as a lawyer friend had told her, was evidence of guilt.

Twice she tapped out the number that the information operator had given her, but both times she hung up before the connection was complete. She went to the kitchen and gulped down a glass of water. Her hands felt clammy. The third time, she let the call go through.

"Is this 268-5125?" she responded to an abrupt hello.

"Who is this?"

She consulted her prepared statement.

"Let's just say that I am Myra Wahl's avenger." On the other end, there was a sharp intake of breath. My God, I am right, she thought. "You're not going to get away with Myra's murder. Your time is running out. The police will pick you up before evening."

"What the hell sort of a sick joke is this?" the voice shrilled.

Joanne Short had exhausted the writing on her sheet but her mind was racing.

"No joke. Or rather, this time the joke's on you. Because we both know you murdered Myra Wahl. I even know about your other crime, though it's Myra I'm avenging."

The voice was suddenly calmer. "Then why are you warning me?"

Joanne Short slammed the receiver down.

Instantly, her heart beating furiously, she took up a sheet and ratcheted it into the typewriter. "Who Murdered Myra Wahl?" she began, a grim smile curving her lips. There was no way Cerezzi could dismiss this. Thirty minutes later she was nearing the bottom of the third page when the doorbell shook her concentration. Still deeply preoccupied, she went out of her study to the front door. All at once a ski-masked face confronted her through the glass on the upper part of the door. Joanne Short opened her mouth to scream. A gun swung up from the intruder's right hand, directed straight at her. Her scream turned into a terrified whimper. Open the door, the gun motioned. For a moment, time seemed to stand still, and Joanne Short was suspended in a state of paralysis. Then, blindly, she whirled toward her study and started to run. Behind her, glass shattered. He was opening the door. Coming in. Coming after her. She reached the study. She struggled to pull the door closed, but a split second later, a foot was wedged firmly in the doorway. Then, with a powerful thrust, the study door burst open. The gun's muzzle pointed straight at her chest.

"I've been watching you."

Nausea gripped Joanne Short. Through the dense fog of unreality that sucked her down, she frantically tried to fathom how this could be. Everything seemed to spin. Then quite suddenly she knew, and her nausea turned to wretching. She doubled over. The intruder watched, the hideous ski mask concealing all expression. The gun motioned her to the couch. Shaken with fear and a terrible sick sense of defeat, she stumbled to obey.

"How did you find out about me?" the intruder demanded.

"I don't know what you're talking about," she stammered, half-crazed with terror.

The intruder stepped forward. A gloved hand rose and slapped her, slamming her back against the cushions. Joanne Short moaned.

"Now—want to tell me how you found out about me?"

She moaned again, but no words came out.

The gun turned in the intruder's hand, its butt facing outward. She felt the crash against her cheek. She was conscious of a searing pain, as if hot irons were sinking deep into her flesh. Blood spurted out from the gash. She coughed. Blood came out of her mouth, then a tooth. Her body slumped to the floor.

The intruder walked over to the desk. Gloved hands picked up two sheets and then yanked the third out of the typewriter. The intruder scanned the sheets, then pocketed them.

"You're very smart and very foolish," the voice said. "Unfortunately, Reverend, that's a fatal combination."

Thursday Evening

The buzzer sounded in Daniel's office. He put down his pen, sighed, and lifted the receiver. "Yes, Pat."

"Janet Karp is here."

So soon, he thought. Barely an hour had passed since Ruth Karp had told him where her daughter was staying. Then he had called the hotel, the Malibu Inn, and left an urgent message for Janet. But now he felt unprepared. He hadn't expected the girl to show up without phoning first.

"Show her in," he said. "And hold all calls until we're through, Pat."

With her petite form and delicate features, Janet Karp looked anything but a murderer. The smile she gave Daniel was brief. She chose the old armchair across from his desk, scrunching her body up tightly.

"You told the hotel operator that it was urgent I see you immediately. Why?"

"I have a message . . ."

"From whom?"

"Your father."

For a second Daniel was sure she would jump up and flee. He was wrong. When she spoke, her voice was chilly, the words coming out like darts.

"What is the message?"

"First you should know that your father swore to me he is innocent of Myra Wahl's murder."

"I see. And he wanted you to bring me the good news. What does my dear father think, that I'm going to take back what I told the police?"

Daniel answered levelly, ignoring the rage in her voice. "No, he doesn't expect you to do that. But your father believes that you know he's innocent."

"How would I know that, Rabbi?"

"Your father," Daniel continued, "thinks that you murdered Myra Wahl and framed him."

"Is that what he told you?" Her voice was icy cold. "He is unbelievable." Her slender fingers gripped the side of the armchair.

"Then there's no truth in what he said?"

Janet Karp stood up and leaned over his desk, her pretty face distorted with the intensity of her words. "*My father murdered Myra Wahl.*"

"Are you so sure?" Daniel asked. Abruptly, extreme weariness swept over him. The day had gone on far too long. In the morning Milton Karp had said his daughter was a murderer; now his daughter was turning the same charge against him. He thought of the God-awful tragedy that had brought a father and daughter to such a hatred. He felt his *koach*, his strength, just ebbing away.

"Of course I'm sure." Janet Karp sat down again in her chair and proceeded to go over the evidence, all of which Daniel knew. "And tell me, Rabbi," she ended finally, her voice brittle with derision, "has my dear father revealed to the police the *truth* about me yet?"

"No. And he's not going to."

"Oh, and why not?"

"That was my message for you. To tell you that he knew what you had done, but that he wasn't going to tell the police anything. He wants you to know that he forgives you."

"The bastard. So he told you I'm a murderer?"

"It's no different from what you're saying about him."

"It is different, Rabbi: *he's* lying. I know it, and he knows that I know it."

"Then explain something to me, Ms. Karp. Why was it so important to your father that I give you this message?"

Her laughter was short and impatient. "That's not hard to figure out. He's trying to manipulate me, like always. Can't you see what's he's doing?"

Daniel shook his head.

"What daughter wants to send her own father to prison, or worse? He's hoping that if he makes me feel guilty, I'll retract." She saw the doubt on Daniel's face. "You probably think I'm a bad daughter, don't you?"

"I didn't say that."

"But you think it." She scanned the tall, cluttered bookshelves. "All these books think it, too, don't they? What does Judaism say about a daughter who testifies against her own father?"

"Jewish law doesn't allow children to testify for or against their parents. The parent-child relationship is too emotional, both for good and bad. Things could be invented, or at the very least exaggerated."

"Are you suggesting I made up or exaggerated what I heard?"

"No, but—"

"You're damn right, no. I'm not out on any vendetta to get my father. Just the opposite. I came down to LA all the way from Seattle, twelve hundred miles, and you know why?" The tortured emotion on her young face silenced him. "To make up with my father." Her eyes darkened with pain. "I hadn't seen him or spoken to him in over a year. And then a man just like you, a rabbi up in Seattle, convinced me I had to make peace. And after a year, what happens? My mother sends me to find him at the temple, and before we even speak I hear him saying those awful, awful things to Myra. And right then and there, I remembered why I hated him. And I ran. I couldn't stand the thought of seeing him. But as angry as I was, at Myra as well as at him, I want you to know something. It never entered my mind that Myra's death was anything but an accident. Until I heard your show on Tuesday. That's when I realized that his threat and Myra's death were no coincidence." Her voice broke off, and she sat still, staring at his shelves. The seconds ticked by. Finally, Daniel leaned over and switched on his desk lamp. The light seemed to startle her. Then she said hoarsely, "So you still think I shouldn't have gone to the police?"

"I don't know. All I can tell you is this: your father may be a murderer, and he may hate you as much as you think you hate him. But it that's the case, he's the greatest actor I've ever seen. Because the man I spoke to this morning loves his daughter." The buzzer sounded again on Daniel's desk, and he picked up the receiver. "Pat," he said, before his secretary could get in a word, "I asked you to hold all calls."

He slammed the phone down. A second later it buzzed again. He ignored it. There was a knock on the door. He strode over, wondering what had possessed Pat Hastings. But when he flung the door open, it was not Pat, but Brenda Goldstein, who confronted him. She marched into the room and then stopped short, startled at Janet Karp's presence, taking in the tear-stained face and rigid shoulders. Daniel clenched his hands. What's Cerezzi going to get me for now, he thought, tampering with a prosecution witness?

"How long have you been here?" Brenda asked Janet Karp, ignoring Daniel.

"About a half hour."

"And where were you before you got here?"

"With friends. Why?"

Brenda turned to Daniel, her tone clipped and professional. "Where have you been this afternoon?"

"I've been right here in the synagogue since noon. Why?"

"You haven't gone out at all?"

"No. Why?"

"Because between one-thirty and four this afternoon, Joanne Short was murdered."

"Who is Joanne Short?" Janet Karp broke the stunned silence.

"A friend of Myra Wahl's," Brenda answered. "At one-thirty this afternoon, Short telephoned Cerezzi and told him she knew who the murderer was. She refused to give Cerezzi the name, insisting that if he'd come see her she could explain everything. He got to her house just over an hour ago. She was dead, shot three times in the head and chest at very close range."

"That means my . . . fa . . . father was under arrest when she was murdered?" the girl stammered.

"Yes. He still is for that matter, but my guess is he'll be

released any minute. You know, it might sound like a funny thing to say, but in a way your father is lucky he was arrested for Myra Wahl's murder—he's now the one person with an ironclad alibi for the time of Joanne Short's death."

"So my father's innocent?" Janet Karp asked, a tremor in her voice.

"Yes. As a matter of fact, the one specific thing Joanne Short would tell Cerezzi was that we were holding the wrong man." Brenda smiled sympathetically at Janet. "Remember what I said to you in my office, that it all might turn out to be a terrible coincidence?"

Janet Karp did not return her smile, but stared straight ahead, her eyes blank. Brenda looked to Daniel for an explanation, but to his relief a loud knock on the door spared him from giving one. Pat Hastings came in, holding out the final edition of the *Times*. "I'm leaving now," she said, "but I thought you'd want to see this." She had folded the paper to isolate the bottom left columns: "Synagogue President Charged in Murder of Rabbi." An incongruous photo of a smiling Milton Karp accompanied the text. After a glance at Brenda, Daniel started to read aloud.

"A Jewish communal leader was charged today with last Sunday night's murder of Rabbi Myra Wahl, who was struck and killed while jogging at midnight on Gateway Avenue.

"The arrested man, Milton Karp, is president of the Pico Boulevard Temple, where Wahl served as associate rabbi. Karp currently serves as chairman of the board of West Coast Construction.

"Lieutenant Joseph Cerezzi of the LAPD, in charge of the investigation, refused to elaborate on possible motives for the homicide, stating, 'All will come out in due course. In the meantime, we have compelling evidence linking Mr. Karp to the murder vehicle.'

"At this time, no bail has been set."

The article continued inside. Daniel kept on reading aloud, but then suddenly winced. A sidebar on page five proclaimed a scoop—the story of Karp's prison sentence in Illinois. "Oh my God," Janet cried, snatching the paper from his fingers.

Daniel turned to Brenda, his voice tight with anger. "Still think Milton Karp's a lucky man?"

"What can I say?" she shrugged. "You know the case we had against him. How could we not have arrested him?"

"And what about the objections I offered Cerezzi? You saw how he reacted. He didn't even want to listen."

"Don't be so sensitive. Put yourself in the lieutenant's shoes—I'm sure you'd have done the exact same thing." Daniel was not appeased. "I know I would have."

Janet Karp moaned. "I've ruined my father," she said.

Brenda went over to Janet and bent to her eye level.

"Look, Janet, first of all, your father's not ruined." She took the *Times* out of the girl's limp hand. "By tomorrow they'll be using this paper to wrap fish."

"*You don't understand anything.*" The girl was obviously on the verge of hysteria. "For the last thirty years, my father has lived in utter terror that people would find out about his prison sentence. Ten years ago they wanted to make him president of the temple and he refused. He was afraid to be in the public eye. When he took it two years ago, my mother told me it was only because he finally felt safe." She pulled the newspaper back and shook it. "It's all my fault. I want to die."

"Listen to me, Janet." Daniel's voice was calm now and firm. "I'm not going to tell you your father's lucky. He's not. But there's one thing I can tell you. At this moment you have a lot more reason to be happy than to be sad."

Janet Karp stared wildly at Daniel.

"Listen to me. Less than one hour ago, you walked into this office, convinced that your father was a killer. I didn't hear you say anything then about wanting to die. Now you find out your father's innocent, and suddenly you're plunged into the deepest depression. Does that make any sense at all?"

"What's the matter with you people?" She glared at them with burning, reproachful eyes. "Don't you understand? Everything that happened is my fault."

"*It is not.* Twelve hours before she was murdered, you

overheard your father threaten Myra Wahl. It's not your fault that you heard him, and it's not your fault that you thought he might be involved in her death. Almost anyone would have reached the same conclusion."

"But don't you see?" Janet said, her voice going weak. "It's only because of what I told Myra that he threatened her."

For a few seconds Daniel was quiet. "Granted that you shouldn't have told Myra that," he said gently, "but the bigger wrongs were done by her and your father: *she* used information given to her in confidence; *he* retaliated by threatening her with bodily harm."

She rose and reached blindly for her coat. "Nice try, Rabbi. But this is one bridge I've burned. There's no way my father's ever going to forgive me. You know better than I what he thinks of me."

He moved to her side. "You know, Janet, you and your father have some very foolish ideas about each other. But he loves you very much. Just go and speak with him. You'll see, he'll forgive you."

"I'm afraid to see him."

Daniel had a sudden flash of inspiration. "Promise me one thing, that you'll come to services here Shabbat morning."

The girl managed a wan smile. "It's a little late for that, Rabbi. What do you want me to pray, that two plus two will equal five?"

"Please promise me, Janet, that you'll be here. In the meantime, I'll talk to your father. Don't worry, we'll work something out."

"You really think so?" Her eyes held a sudden glimmer of hope.

"I do," he said.

The girl held out her hand shyly. Daniel took it. "Thank you," she whispered and hurried out.

Brenda raised her eyebrows at Daniel. "What are you planning for Saturday morning, Rabbi?"

"Come to shul and find out." She grimaced, and he grinned at her. "I'll use *any* means to get Jews into synagogue."

She laughed. "You know, watching you in action just now

was a revelation. I never realized to what extent psychologists and rabbis are in the same business. You really handled that quite well, Rabbi Daniel Winter."

Daniel gave a mock bow. "And now, Dr. Goldstein, maybe you can tell me why yóu hotfooted it here with the news?"

"Who said I came directly here?" she flushed.

"You told us when you came in that Cerezzi discovered Joanne Short's body a little over an hour ago. That means about four o'clock. I somehow doubt that you were the first person he called. First he would have to bring out other cops, lab people and all that. So my guess is that he didn't call you before a quarter to five. And you were here twenty minutes later." He watched with amusement as her green eyes widened. "I'm right, aren't I?"

"You don't miss a trick, do you?"

Daniel waited.

"When Cerezzi called me—and by the way it was four thirty-five, Sherlock—he asked me a disturbing question. Did Daniel Winter know it was Joanne Short who gave the police the information about his fight with Myra Wahl Sunday night? I had to tell him the truth. I know Cerezzi, Daniel. This time he's not going to let go. He'll demand to know where you were last Sunday night, and for that matter, where you were today."

"I've told you already, I've hardly been out of my office since noon. You can ask Pat Hastings."

"Daniel," she said in exasperation, "it's less than a ten minute drive from here to Joanne Short's house." She marched over to the other end of the office, her cheeks flaming, and pulled the back door open. "You could have left at any time by this door without being seen. Could Pat Hastings swear that she saw you or spoke with you at intervals of no more than twenty-five minutes?"

His mouth tightened a fraction. "No," he shook his head. "She couldn't. Pat herself was out on an errand between two and three o'clock."

"Which means that in theory you could have walked out this door, climbed into your car, and returned twenty-five minutes later with no one the wiser. Don't look at me like that, Daniel. I like you. A lot. That's why I let you intimidate me the last time I tried to question you. Believe me, I didn't do you any favor. Everything I'm asking you now, Cerezzi's going to ask. Only he's gong to be a lot more unpleasant about it."

Daniel nodded. "I understand." He reflected for a few minutes. Then incongruously he smiled. "So you like me a *lot?*"

"Daniel, this is serious."

"I am serious, Brenda. I like you, too, and I trust you. And believe me, where I was Sunday night is totally irrelevant to Myra's death. But I'll tell you about it."

"Good." She breathed a sigh and sat down.

"But I'll have to speak first with the party in question."

"Cut the euphemisms, Daniel," Brenda snapped. "I'm not an adolescent with a crush, and I don't own you. So let's start all over. The party in question is a woman, right?"

"A married women, Brenda. Nothing wrong happened between us. You must believe that. When I left you Sunday night all I wanted was to go home and be alone. But when I got there, she . . . the woman . . . was parked in front of my house. Brenda, if her husband knows we saw each other, it would be very bad."

"For whom?"

"For her, more than for me. But for me, too," he conceded. He tried to decipher her face, which was half in shadow. "Do you believe me, that nothing happened?" There was an uncharacteristic hesitation in his voice.

"Yes, Daniel," she said, her voice softer now. She had exhausted her anger with her outburst. "But why didn't you level with us from the beginning? We would have handled the whole thing discreetly."

"With the same discretion with which you handled Milton Karp's affairs?"

Brenda grimly acknowledged the rebuke. "So you're going to speak with her?"

"Yes."

"When?"

"Tomorrow night I'll explain everything to you."

"When?" she repeated stubbornly.

"When you come with Jessica to my house for Shabbat

dinner." Her stern expression melted before Daniel's infectious smile. "Services are at five, and we'll eat afterward. Can you make it?"

She nodded.

Brenda had hardly left Daniel's office before he raced back to his desk. He rummaged through his papers until he found what he wanted. Then he lifted the receiver and dialed a New York City number. A familiar voice answered.

"Ms. Rand?" he asked.

"Yes." She paused. "It's you, Rabbi Winter, right?"

"Yes."

"What do you want?"

"To know if you were back in New York."

"Why? Have you told the police about me?"

"No."

"Then what do you want?" She was defensive. He could understand why, and was only sorry to be the cause of it.

"I wanted to know where to reach you, in case of emergency."

"Okay. Well, now you know."

"Yes. Thank you."

Silence.

"They haven't caught anyone yet, have they?"

"No."

"Will you call me if they do?"

"Yes."

"Good night, then. I'm sorry if I sounded annoyed."

After hanging up, he pondered the face of his watch and made some rapid calculations. The earliest Joanne Short could have been killed was a few minutes after one-thirty. Barely five hours ago. There was no way Evelyn Rand could now be in New York if she had been in LA five hours earlier. No way at all—was there? He smiled with relief. His instinct about her had been right all along. Good that he hadn't gone to the police. Good that he could still trust his instincts.

One unpleasant call down, one to go. He sighed, flipped open his telephone book, and dialed. To his considerable relief, the voice he was silently praying for was the one that answered.

"Do you recognize me?" he asked. "If so, just say yes."

"Yes."

"Is your husband, or anybody else, with you?"

"No."

"Good." He breathed deeply. "I don't know where to start, Leah, but some terrible things have been happening. Sunday night, while we were together, Myra Wahl was murdered."

"I know."

"Of course," he said, remembering that her husband and Myra were cousins. "Well, just before I saw you that evening I'd had a terrible fight with Myra."

"I know, Daniel, I heard it on the air."

"That's right, but it got worse after the show. Anyway, the police are demanding I tell them where I was until one o'clock that morning."

"What are you talking about? They've arrested Milton Karp. I heard it on the news."

He told her that Karp was about to be released. "Now *I'm* under suspicion."

"That's the most ridiculous thing I've ever heard."

"Is it? An hour after I yell at Myra that I won't forgive her, she's murdered. The police naturally want to know where I was when she died."

"And what did you tell them?"

"That I was with someone whose identity could not be disclosed."

"*I don't believe you, Daniel.* Why in heaven's name didn't you just say you were home alone?"

"I assure you, it wouldn't have helped. I don't want to go into the whole thing now, but by a weird coincidence someone from the police department was trying to reach me Sunday night. They know I wasn't home."

"What are you planning?" Her voice slipped from anger to fright.

"I need to give them your name."

"No!"

"Leah, we did nothing wrong—"

"I know that, and you know that. But you know Ronnie won't believe us. As it is, he's already suspicious."

"Of what? He told me at the funeral he was out of town Sunday night."

"And he apparently spent it checking up on me. He called here at ten-thirty Sunday night and we spoke. That's why I went out later—I thought I was safe. But he called again at midnight and at one and left messages on the machine." She broke off in dismay. "When he didn't find me at home, Daniel, he phoned your house. He's been making snide remarks the whole week, and of course I've denied everything. But know this, Daniel, if I give you an alibi for Sunday night and he finds out, my marriage is over, kaput."

"Leah, I swear to you. I've done everything possible to keep your name out of it. I just can't any longer." He told her about Joanne Short's murder and the pressure Cerezzi was putting on him.

"Tell me, is Ronnie leaving town again soon?"

"He's flying to Portland Sunday afternoon."

"Could you speak with the police *then?*"

"Are you in real danger, Daniel?"

"If you don't speak up, I am."

"And you swear to me that there's no way Ronnie will ever find out?"

"I can't swear that, Leah. In matters like this, there's always a risk, but I really do believe it's a very small one."

She was silent a long while. "I don't want the police coming to my house. My neighbors are a bunch of busybodies."

"That can be arranged."

"And it can't be before five on Sunday."

"I'll tell Lieutenant Cerezzi. I think I can hold him off until Sunday evening."

"And Daniel, I don't want the cops phoning here."

"I'll tell him."

"I'll do it, Daniel. You know why?" He could hear the bitterness in her voice. "Because I love you, dammit. What do you think of that?"

She hung up before he could say a word.

Friday Afternoon

Pat Hastings rapped once on the door and entered Daniel's office. She was wearing a pale-blue overcoat, and her purse was slung over her shoulder.

"Wish me a good weekend," she announced grandly. "Norm and I are taking the kids sailing."

"Isn't it a little early to be leaving, though?"

Pat looked at him quizzically. "It's Friday." During the winter months, when the Sabbath started between four and five, the synagogue office closed early on Friday afternoons.

A self-conscious smile spread across Daniel's face. "Of course," he said, tousling his hair absentmindedly. "Forgive me, Pat. I must really be distracted."

"Thinking about the murders?"

He nodded.

"Lieutenant Cerezzi called while you were at lunch."

"What did he want?"

"To speak to me." Seeing his surprise, she explained, "He asked if I'd seen you yesterday, when, that sort of stuff." Daniel said nothing. "I can't believe it. Does he really think you might be involved in that Reverend Short's murder?"

"I don't know what he thinks, Pat."

"Well, *I know what I think*. I told him he had some nerve. A maniac killer is loose in this city, and he's wasting his time pestering one of our leading rabbis."

Daniel laughed, in spite of his fatigue. "And what did the lieutenant say to that?"

"The nerve of that man," Pat grumbled. "He laughed. Then he said he liked loyal employees and that if I ever needed another job he hoped I would keep the LAPD in mind. I told him that if things ever came to such a pass, he would be my second choice. And he fell right in. 'Oh, and who's your first?' he asked. I told him, 'Everybody else.'"

Daniel laughed out loud. "Pat, you're great. I needed that."

"Oh, by the way, a few things before I leave. Don't forget, you have a wedding here tomorrow night at eight. Marcia Diskin and Daryl Kelman. You've been doing so many weddings recently, I hope you remember who they are."

"I sure do," said Daniel. He thought back to his meeting with Daryl Kelman and inwardly suppressed a groan.

"While you were at lunch, Bartley Turner called from KLAX. He left an odd message, so let me read it to you exactly. 'The timetable's been moved up. We need an answer by Monday.' Does that make sense to you?"

Daniel nodded. One more pressure, he thought.

"Anything else?"

"That's it." She started through the door and then abruptly looked back. "Please don't let this stuff get you down, Daniel. You're a good guy, and you deserve better."

"Thanks, Pat, you're a gem."

After she left, he stayed at his desk, brooding. He thought of Bartley Turner's message. On top of all the tension of the murder investigations, he now had seventy-two hours in which to decide the future direction of his life. And yet . . . ? If he had to call Turner at this moment, he was almost sure he would tell him, "Hold everything. I'm coming." And forget about the Daryl Kelmans of this world, and about all those kids who would save a drowning dog before a drowning stranger, and about the bar mitzvah student who stole Brenda's watch, and about Wilbur Kantor, who any day now would undoubtedly revert to his old sarcastic self. He thought of the last week, of the two women he had known, now dead, and of the emotional load that Milton and Janet Karp had dumped on him—"Yessir," he muttered, "that radio show is starting to sound better and better."

* * *

Captain Robert Grier was furious, his long, furrowed face contorted. He leaned across his deak and waved a batch of telegrams at Joe Cerezzi.

"American Jewish Committee, American Jewish Congress, the Jewish Welfare Federation, the Union of American Hebrew Congregations—get the picture, Lieutenant? Here, listen to this one: 'Dear Mr. Mayor, The Union of American Hebrew Congregations, the offical organ of Reform temples, protests the false arrest of one of our distinguished leaders, Mr. Milton Karp. The release of Mr. Karp only hours after being charged points either to shoddy police work or to an act of harassment. We assume that appropriate measures will be taken against the responsible party.'" The captain flung the messages down on his immaculate white desk and made a visible effort to restrain himself. "The others aren't quite so blunt about firing you, Lieutenant, but the general tone is, let's just say, not friendly."

Cerezzi sat impassively, his dark eyes narrowed.

"And the mayor is *pissed*, Lieutenant. His Honor is is in a very tight race this coming November, and he somehow got the notion in his head that Jews contribute more money to political campaigns than Italian police lieutenants. Follow what I'm saying? And the mayor, with his unerring political instinct, suspects that Jewish people will not be well disposed toward mayors whose police officials casually and wrongly arrest their leaders for murder."

"Captain, that's a low blow, and you know it." Mechanically, Cerezzi listed all the factors that had led to Milton Karp's arrest, checking them off one by one on his fingers. "If you were in charge of the investigation, would you have acted any different?"

"I would have gone over it piece by piece with my captain," Grier snapped. "Common sense, Lieutenant. This isn't picking up some dope dealer in Watts or some fag with a knife in West Hollywood. This is a very prominent man in the Jewish community, and Jews are damned sensitive people." He closed his eyes and breathed heavily. "Now, who are your other suspects?"

Cerezzi coughed. "At this point in time, Captain, we

. . . have very little to go on." He started to detail the case against Daniel Winter, the rabbi's refusal to give an alibi for Sunday night, and the reasons he had for being furious both at Myra Wahl and Joanne Short. "On the other hand, I've spent some time with him, and I'm ninety-nine point nine percent sure that he's okay. But I would like to hear his alibi."

"Okay. But given the political climate right now, don't lean on him too much, unless you're sure he's the one."

"What does 'sure' mean, Captain? How often are we one hundred percent sure?"

Grier ignored him. "Any other suspects?"

Cerezzi told Grier about the threatening phone call directed against both Wahl and Short on the radio show Sunday night. The captain scowled as he digested the information, stroking his mustache.

"Any leads on that, Lieutenant?"

"So far, no. It's damned hard trying to trace a call like that."

Grier sighed with infinite weariness. "Do you have anything else to report?" His voice was dangerously patient.

Cerezzi described the note to Rabbi Wahl Daniel had discovered and his suspicion that the writer had been a rejected female lover. The captain groaned melodramatically. "Jeez—every which way we look at it, the Jews are going to be in an uproar over this one. Listen, get me a written report on the investigation. Maybe something will occur to me." He paused and appeared lost in thought. "Now, what's this I hear about the Short murder, that the reverend phoned just before she was killed. Is that true?"

While Cerezzi filled him in on the call, Grier swung his chair around and glowered out the window. The sky had gone a poisonous gray. It was going to pour soon.

"Let me tell you something, Lieutenant. With all due respect, you've been *sloppy*. When somebody, a minister, for God's sake, waves a flag at you like that, you scuttle right out and see them."

"It's easy to be a Monday morning quarterback, Captain," Cerezzi said evenly, but his eyes were dark with anger. "With the case we had against Karp, I think you would have acted just like I did."

Grier tugged at his mustache. "Possibly, Lieutenant. Maybe you acted logically. Unfortunately, however, these murders are following a logic we don't understand yet." He cocked an eye sarcastically. "Any good news for me on your third case? Brine. Any suspects there?"

"We think it's the husband, Elmer Brine."

"Great. A nice normal homicide. Man kills wife. No rabbis, no priests, no nuns. You got a motive?"

"Not yet. The guy's got a record. Nothing major. Penny-ante stuff."

Grier nodded and cleared his throat. "Well, I guess that's about it for today."

Cerezzi rose stiffly and started for the door.

"One last thought, Joe. You've got three unsolved murders, and two—maybe three—murderers wandering around loose out there. The city wants them solved yesterday, the mayor wants them solved yesterday, and the department wants them solved yesterday. And remember, Lieutenant, it's only February."

"So?" Cerezzi looked back at him, eyebrows raised.

"So that means you've used up your quota of false arrests for the rest of the year."

Cerezzi opened the door slowly to the sound of Grier's chuckle. "Oh, one last thing." Cerezzi turned round again. A thin-lipped smile adorned the captain's face. "Have a nice weekend, Lieutenant."

Daniel dialed the Karp residence. After a series of busy signals, the line finally cleared. Ruth Karp answered. Her voice was euphoric.

"This is Rabbi Daniel Winter. May I please speak with Milton Karp?"

"Oh, Rabbi Winter, hello. How good to hear from you. I'm sorry, my husband is sleeping, and after these last two days, I really don't want to wake him. Is it important?"

"Yes," Daniel said. "But I think you can help me. When is the main Sabbath service at the Pico Boulevard Temple?"

Ruth Karp's laughter was musical. "Is that what you called to ask, Rabbi? Are you thinking of turning Reform?"

"Not just yet, Mrs. Karp," Daniel joined in her laughter. "But seriously, when is your main service, Friday night or Saturday?"

"Friday night, Rabbi, is when we get our big crowd. Being as he's the president, Milton and I always make sure to be there. Saturday morning, on the other hand, we're lucky if we get even ten people for a minyan. But why do you want to know?"

Daniel breathed a sigh of relief. "I would like to invite you both, but your husband in particular, to join us at my shul on Saturday morning."

"But why?"

"Did Mr. Karp tell you about the conversation we had Thursday morning?"

"He did, Rabbi. He was terribly impressed by you, said you helped him a lot. As a matter of fact, he said you also gave him some advice that helped him with the police."

"Did he say anything about your daughter?"

Her voice was suddenly guarded, older. "We know that it was Janet who informed on Milt, if that's what you're getting at."

"Has she been in touch with you?"

"No, Rabbi. I think she realizes it would be inappropriate right now. After what she's done."

"Let me ask you something, Mrs. Karp. From my talk with your husband I gather that he and Janet have a very tense relationship. Is that true?"

"Ye-es."

"And I gather that Mr. Karp feels responsible for this tension. True?"

"It was true in the past, but . . ."

"So let me ask you something. Do the two of you want to make peace with your daughter?"

"She tried to get him convicted of *murder*, Rabbi." Her voice shook with emotion. "Don't we have the right to be angry?"

"You know the circumstantial evidence that the police had

against your husband. Can't you understand why Janet was suspicious?"

"But to turn in her own father? Listen, you're a rabbi, is that Jewish ethics?"

"Let me ask you again. Do you want peace with your daughter?"

"No." Her voice was sullen, but emphatic.

"Mrs. Karp, if Janet were killed . . ."

"God forbid!"

"If Janet were killed, would you go to the funeral?"

"Of course—"

"So you're waiting for her to die before you'll make peace with her?"

"What are you planning, Rabbi?"

"Please make sure he joins us for services tomorrow. Okay?"

"Okay." Her voice was subdued, but he knew she would do what he asked.

"And Shabbat Shalom."

"What did you say, Rabbi?"

"A happy and peaceful Sabbath to you and Mr. Karp."

He put the phone down. A smile curved the corners of his mouth.

En route to his office, Lieutenant Joe Cerezzi did three things: slammed his fist against a wall, maligned the antecedents of a certain captain, and generally resolved that someday he'd be chief of police and bust Robert Grier back to walking a beat. It was in this genial frame of mind that he greeted Doris Touhey, Brenda Goldstein's secretary, who was waiting outside his office, unwrapping a stick of gum.

"What do you want?" he said brusquely, striding past her into the office and catching, as usual, the pungent scent of her perfume.

"I need to speak to you, Lieutenant," she said, undeterred, trailing him inside. She crumpled the foil and tossed it deftly in his ashtray.

He grabbed a batch of telephone messages. "You and the

rest of the world," he growled. Doris Touhey didn't budge. "Can't it wait?"

She shook her head energetically.

He eased his large frame into his battered stuffed chair. "I'm bushed, Doris. This better be important."

"I think it is," she said in a stubborn, serious voice that put him on the immediate alert.

"Shoot."

"Brenda—Dr. Goldstein—sent down a request to the lab for some stuff; you know, the way she always does." Cerezzi nodded. "Well, a little while ago Dick Phillips called from the lab, all excited. Told me there was a report I should get for Dr. Goldstein immediately." Cerezzi skimmed his own messages. Phillips had phoned him twice in the last ten minutes. Both slips were marked urgent.

Doris Touhey handed him an envelope. Cerezzi ripped it open, read Phillips' report, and let out a low whistle. "Had Brenda seen this yet?"

"She's gone for the day, Lieutenant."

"A little early, isn't it?"

"She's going to Rabbi Winter's synagogue for services. The service starts at five, I think."

"When should she be home then?"

"She's going to the rabbi's for dinner, Lieutenant. She left the address and phone number, if you need them. I wrote them down for you."

Cerezzi took the slip of paper and clipped it to the front of the Phillips folder. Despite his exhaustion, his heart was hammering. "Doris, not a word about this to anybody, and I mean *anybody*. That includes Dr. Goldstein, in case she should call. Is that clear?"

She nodded and moved to the door.

Cerezzi's mouth twisted. "Rabbi Winter is going to have an unexpected Sabbath guest this evening."

Friday Evening

Brenda leafed through the prayer book, anxiously seeking the magic words, "Friday Evening Service." No luck. Jessica, she saw, with a slight sense of shame, had quickly located the page. She was hopelessly scanning the table of contents when she heard Daniel's announcement from the pulpit. "Turn to page 126 in your siddur." She looked up gratefully. For a second their eyes met, and she thought she saw the flicker of a smile. Then Daniel cleared his throat.

"The Friday evening service," he began, "starts with six psalms. These psalms, according to one commentary, represent the six preceding days of the week. Therefore, as we recite them tonight, let us go back to the day each psalm stands for and recall what happened to us. And remember, since the Jewish calendar starts at night, the first psalm represents Saturday night to Sunday evening."

Daniel stepped down, and the cantor mounted the pulpit. "*Lekhu Neranenah*," the rich bass voice began. "Come let us praise God." A hum of voices joined in the prayer, whispering their way through the psalmist's exaltation of God. Brenda turned back to her own siddur and had barely worked her way through half of the English translation when the cantor began, "*Shiru*—Let us sing a new song to God." The second psalm already. She recalled Daniel's words—this one applied to Sunday night through Monday. Her thoughts drifted back to Sunday evening: to her first sight of Myra, bursting into the radio station with cheeks flushed, wearing the dark green jogging suit. And to Daniel. How fine he had looked, in a corduroy jacket and tan pants, and how at ease in the ambience of

KLAX. Then to the program, the heated skirmishes over abortion, that wild, threatening call that had given her the shivers, and that desperate woman—what was her name? Lorna, Laura, something like that. She remembered how Myra had jumped up to speak with the woman during the break and how touched she had been by Myra's compassion. It showed another, softer side to Myra, a contrast to the furious one Brenda had seen later. The cantor's voice, "God reigns. Let the earth be glad," sliced through her reverie.

A few minutes later, when the congregation finished singing *Lekha Dodi*—"it's a love song to the Sabbath," Brenda read—Daniel rose again. "Whatever happened these last six days is now in the past. Take a deep breath and let go of it, for now we come to the seventh psalm, the psalm for the Sabbath. With this prayer we turn toward the future, the Sabbath that lies before us."

"That Rabbi Winter," a stooped, elderly woman at Brenda's side whispered, chuckling, "always coming up with some new gimmick."

Brenda felt a lightness in her chest, her shoulders, and then all over her body, and as she breathed out she felt some of the strains of the past week slowly dissipate. She turned back to her prayer book, focusing now on the words, going back and forth between the English and Hebrew. By the time the congregation concluded with *Yigdal* she was quite at ease.

"Shabbat Shalom," Daniel waved to her and Jessica as he emerged into the corridor from the sanctuary. Jessica gripped her mother's arm, talking rapidly and pointing. Her small face was sprinkled liberally with freckles. She had her mother's deep green eyes and wide mouth, but her hair was dark brown and curly. Daniel pushed his way over to them, mechanically shaking the hands stretched out to him. Jessica's friend, Donna Gillis, dragged Jessica away just as he neared them.

"You look very pretty," he told Brenda, mischievously pleased when she blushed. She had indeed taken great care with her appearance. She wore a black silk shirt inside a white wool suit, and high heeled black sandals. A touch of eye shadow set off her green eyes. He was absurdly delighted to see her.

"So how did it feel?" he asked.

"A little bit weird," she admitted. "And a little bit wonderful."

"Is that good?" Daniel asked. He smiled with pleasure, but his voice betrayed his anxiousness. He was surprised at how much he wanted to hear her say yes.

"Well, put it this way. At the beginning it felt more weird. By the end, the wonderful was dominating. Satisfied?"

"Very definitely."

"Now what? Should we go to your house in one car, or should Jessica and I follow in ours?"

"I don't drive on the Sabbath."

A flush spread over Brenda's cheeks. "Excuse me," she said. "I should have known that. But you know, Daniel, that makes no sense to me. The Bible was written thousands of years ago. How could it possibly forbid driving?"

"Well it doesn't mention driving by name, if that's what you mean. But the Bible explicitly forbids igniting a fire, and it would be quite a trick to turn on your ignition without doing that." He teased, "You know, not driving has some pretty positive benefits."

"Like what?"

"Well, for one thing, because religious Jews have to live within walking distance of their synagogues, it means they all live near each other. As a result, their communities stay cohesive."

"Good point." She *was* listening, but she was more acutely aware that he had taken her arm.

"Besides, it makes the Sabbath special. How often do you go anywhere by foot when you can drive? I know I never do. This way we can walk and talk."

As if on cue, Jessica dashed over. "Mom, Rabbi Winter," she panted, looking eagerly from one to the other, "can I walk back with Donna and join you later?"

Her mother agreed, and a delighted Jessica darted away.

The two stood together awkwardly as the crowd thinned, avoiding each other's eyes.

"I'm happy we'll have this time alone—" Daniel began.

"Me, too," Brenda said softly, acutely conscious of the inquisitive glances from the congregants filing noisily past.

"Besides," Daniel went on, as they stepped outside into the cool wet darkness, "it will give us a chance to dispose of the one unpleasant item of business. That way we can enjoy the rest of the evening."

Brenda was silent. Daniel set a quick pace. In the last few days the weather had turned chilly; it was a brisk night for February by Los Angeles standards, and Brenda wound a thick black scarf around her neck and dug her hands deep in her pockets. But Daniel strode on with his coat open, oblivious to the cold.

"After the show," Daniel said, "I was furious and wanted to be alone. I drove straight home. When I got there, a car was in front, waiting. Inside, was Leah Mason Gold, a woman I've known for fifteen years." He glanced back at Brenda, trying to read her face in the dim light. "She and I were once almost engaged."

"Are you in love with her?" Brenda asked, and hastily regretted the question.

"I once was."

"And now?"

Daniel kicked at a stone. "No," he shook his head emphatically. "Not anymore."

He told Brenda of his relationship with Leah; how they met again when he moved to Los Angeles, and of Ronnie Gold's jealousy, and how that had ended all contact between them. "Well, Sunday night, Ronnie was out of town. Leah listened to the program, and when it ended she drove over. She came up to me as I got out of my car and insisted that we had to speak. At first I didn't want to—you know the mood I was in—but she sounded desperate, and you have to understand, I'd been in love—or thought I had—with Leah for so many years. So I got into her car."

Daniel slowed.

"And?" Brenda prompted.

"She asked me straight out—if she and Ronnie got divorced, could anything happen between us?"

"And what did you say?" Brenda forced her voice to stay neutral.

"That I didn't believe we were meant for each other. She said she thought that's what I would answer, but that she needed to hear me say it. For a little while, I guess neither of us said anything, and finally she told me not to worry. She wasn't going to leave Ronnie. That's really all there was to it. We sat in the car and talked some more—I suppose we didn't want to leave on so sad a note. Then she drove off, and I went into my house. It was well after one. Anyway, next thing I knew, it was six-thirty, and you were calling to tell me Myra had been murdered."

"Did you have to be so secretive, Daniel?"

"I don't regret it one bit. You know very well that if I had breathed a word of this to Cerezzi he would have questioned Leah immediately. If Ronnie Gold finds out his wife came to my house at midnight, there will be a disaster. I just pray that when I explain everything to Cerezzi, he'll be discreet."

"He will, Daniel. I promise you that."

"Now there's one thing I need to know. Did you really believe I might have murdered Myra?"

"Daniel, of course I didn't."

"Then why were you so troubled when I refused to give an alibi?"

"I was afraid," she said slowly, "there might be a woman in your life."

Daniel stopped walking and turned to face her. He touched her chin lightly. "Who says there isn't?"

The middle-aged man who stood awkwardly before Cerezzi was short, stocky, and thick-necked. His orange flannel shirt was half out of his pants. Nicotine marks stained his chin and fingers. In his right hand he held a *Los Angeles Times*.

"I'm Julie Domino, Lieutenant," he said gruffly. "I own the Pico-Doheny Newsstand."

"Yes, Mr. Domino. What brings you here?"

The man thrust the paper onto Cerezzi's desk, and stabbed with a stubby finger at the front-page photograph of Reverend Joanne Short.

"That woman came to my newsstand yesterday."

"At what time?"

"How can I remember—maybe nine or ten A.M."

"Had she ever been there before?"

"I don't know. She was not a regular, I can tell you that."

"Mr. Domino. You don't remember what time she came. You don't know if you'd ever seen her before." Cerezzi tapped his pen against the picture. "Are you positive that the woman you saw yesterday was Joanne Short?"

"Oh, it was her, all right. There's no way I'd forget her."

"Why?"

"You see, yesterday was Thursday."

Cerezzi swallowed a groan. What other amazing revelations would this man come up with?

"Anyway, people who come to my shop want Thursday's papers on Thursday. Right?" He waited for the lieutenant's assenting nod. "But not this lady. First, I spot her outside, trying to yank the bottom paper from the stack. So I run out and ask her what she wants. Monday's paper, she says. Anyway, I find one under the counter, which makes her real happy." He squinted at the lieutenant. "That seems pretty odd, doesn't it? I mean, seeing as she was murdered a few hours later." Cerezzi's face betrayed nothing. "Don't you think so?"

"Maybe."

"Well, what's the story, was it a waste of time for me to come down here, or what?"

"Mr. Domino, whenever a homicide occurs, we want to speak to everyone who had any contact with the victim on the day of the murder. I can't tell you yet if this has any significance, but we are grateful to you for coming in with this information."

"Thank you, Lieutenant." His dignity satisfied, Julie Domino tucked in his shirt and waddled out of the room. Cerezzi waited until he heard the door of his outer office close.

Then he made a grab for the phone. Seconds later, he was speaking to Ted Castle at the city desk of the *Times*.

"Ted," he said. "Joe Cerezzi."

"Yeah, Joe. Any fresh corpses you want to give me a scoop on?" Before moving to the city desk, Castle had covered homicide for five years.

"I need a small favor, Ted. I need a copy of every edition of this past Monday's papers. Okay?"

"On to something hot?"

Cerezzi said nothing.

"What's my quid pro quo, Joe?"

"When we break the case, you get it first. Deal?"

"Fair enough."

"In the meantime, Castle, do me another favor."

"You've used up your quota, Lieutenant."

Cerezzi ignored the gibe. "Don't waste time trying to figure out what we're after. When the time comes, I'll tell you."

"But first, Joe. Remember."

"First," Cerezzi promised. "In the meantime, get those papers together. I'll be by in twenty minutes."

A gleaming white cloth was spread over the long oak table. In the mirror across from the table, the light was reflected from the two giant silver candlesticks in the opposite corner of the room, sending a glow over the table. At the head of the table, a deep blue velvet cloth, decorated with white embroidered Hebrew words, covered the two challot.

Daniel stood at the head of the table and raised the wine cup. He looks really striking, Brenda thought, in his Sabbath best, the dark gray suit, white shirt, and blue-gray tie.

He began chanting the kiddush, after which he drank from his cup and shared the wine with Brenda and Jessica. Then they followed him into the kitchen. Daniel filled a large cup with water and poured it three times over his right hand and then three times over his left. "Not for hygienic reasons," he told Jessica, and glanced over his shoulder at Brenda. "According to Jewish law, your hands have to be clean before this washing. It's to add a spiritual dimension to the meal we're about to eat." Brenda watched with amusement as her daughter drank in the rabbi's words, her green eyes focused solemnly on him. They moved back into the dining room. He lifted the cloth cover off the two challot, and picked up one. "*Barukh ata,*" he began, "Blessed are You, Lord our God, King of the universe, who brings forth bread from the earth." Jessica followed along eagerly in Hebrew. Brenda repeated the blessing stumblingly—she had known it once, back in her childhood, she thought with a pang. Daniel passed a piece of challah to both of them.

Brenda rose to help Daniel bring in the soup. "Thanks," he said firmly, "but you're my guests. There's no need."

"Maybe you're not such a male chauvinist pig after all," Brenda teased as he came back carefully balancing the steaming plates of soup.

"Mom," Jessica rebuked her, shocked. "You don't speak like that to him. He's a rabbi."

"It's all right, Jessica," Daniel laughed. He sat down after serving them with mock waiter-like efficiency. "The truth of the matter is, all I ever said was, I think there should be some role differences in religion."

"Then what about the other things Myra said Sunday night?" Brenda asked.

"Like what?"

"Like the blessing that religious men make every morning thanking God they're not women."

"I don't make that blessing," Daniel.

"*You* don't?" Jessica called out, with a comical expression of horror. "But you're a *rabbi.*"

"That blessing has bothered me for years, even though I think it's a lot less sexist than the way it sounds now. You see, it was written at a time when a high percentage of women died giving birth. Childbirth was considered so dangerous that Jewish law stated a father could compel his son to get married, but never his daughter, because no woman should be forced to go through childbirth."

"Don't change the subject," Brenda objected. "Why did you stop saying the blessing?"

He broke off a piece of bread. "Because today very few

women die in childbirth, and without that association all we're left with is a blessing that makes men feel superior and women feel bad."

"Can you do that, Rabbi?" Jessica asked, her face solemn. "Just drop a law because you don't like it?"

"Not usually, Jessica. On the other hand, there are very old Jewish sources, containing alternate versions of some of the blessings we still say. Fifteen hundred years ago already there were rabbis who were troubled by the negative phrasing of that blessing. So they reformulated it in a positive form, thanking God that we are free-born Jews."

"So you just changed it?" Jessica was impressed.

"Actually, my natural instincts are very conservative, and so it wasn't easy for me to make the decision. Then one day, a few years ago, I read an article called 'Women in Judaism,' by an old teacher of mine from the Yeshiva. I called him up and asked him straight out, "Rebbe, how can you say that blessing about women?" He answered quietly, "I don't." He hadn't mentioned that in the article because he was afraid he'd get attacked. That's when I decided to stop saying it, too."

"But that's not the only problem," said Brenda. "Isn't it true that among Orthodox Jews, women are given an inferior education to men?"

"It's true," Daniel conceded. "Though among the modern Orthodox, the situation is changing. But let me ask you something, Brenda, isn't it true that the average Orthodox woman, for all that she's supposedly ignorant, knows a lot more about Judaism than the average male Reform Jew?"

And so the evening went on, the talk and laughter breaking off only when Daniel called their attention back to the meal. So this is what Shabbat really means, Brenda thought.

The peace was interrupted by a sharp pounding. With a puzzled look at Brenda, Daniel went to answer the door. Guests rarely came over unannounced at this hour. Puzzlement turned to coldness when he opened the door.

"Hello, Rabbi." Joe Cerezzi extended a hand. He saw Daniel's face tighten. "Please pardon me for interrupting your

Sabbath, Rabbi. I assure you this has nothing to do with your alibi."

"What is it then, Lieutenant?"

"I understand Dr. Goldstein is here. I need to speak with her."

Daniel shrugged and led him into the dining room. Brenda looked up in surprise.

"How did you know I was here?"

"Doris told me. Brenda, I have some shocking news for you."

"What is it, Joe?" Even in the soft candlelight, both men saw the color drain from her face.

Cerezzi took an envelope out of his pocket. "Late this afternoon, Dick Phillips sent this report up from the lab. Brenda, the gun that killed Joanne Short is the same gun that killed your parents."

Saturday Morning

Daniel had just signaled for the congregation to rise for the reading of the Ten Commandments, the highlight of that week's Torah portion, when he felt a tug at the fringes of his prayer shawl.

"Rabbi," Wilbur Kantor hissed, "you're not going to believe who just walked in here."

Daniel looked toward the entrance of the synagogue. Stiffly and slowly, Milton Karp was walking forward, coat clutched in one arm, prayer book and Torah in the other.

"How do you figure that, Rabbi?"

Daniel nodded at Kantor, but said nothing. Bad enough that I'm not concentrating on the Torah reading, he thought. Worse yet if I start a conversation. A moment later, the reader finished chanting the Ten Commandments, the congregation resumed their seats, and Daniel turned to Kantor. But the man had hurried away, and presently Daniel saw him forming a one-man welcoming committee for Milton Karp.

Automatically, Daniel's eyes sought out Janet. From his vantage point on the pulpit, he had spotted her when she entered the synagogue promptly at nine, and he had been checking periodically to make sure she was still there. She was sitting quietly and alone, her attention focused on the volume of the Torah she was holding. If she had noticed her father's entrance, she gave no indication.

The reader resumed the chanting of the Torah portion, and Daniel forced himself to concentrate. But it was no use. His thoughts kept flashing back to the previous night. Only one detail stood out: Ted and Jean Kaplan had been murdered with the same gun that had killed Joanne Short on Thursday. Until well after midnight, Brenda, Daniel, and Cerezzi had sat together, united in their bewilderment. Jessica had begun to sob and eventually fell asleep, tucked into the secure curve of her mother's arm. There was little else Cerezzi could tell them. Oh, yes, Janet Karp's alibi for the time of Joanne Short's death checked out. No question. And yes, even though Daniel's alibi would still have to be verified, this latest discovery, certainly in Cerezzi's eyes, had incontrovertibly removed him as a suspect. And for reasons none of them could figure out, Joanne Short had spent Thursday morning looking for Monday's edition of the *Los Angeles Times*.

Impatiently, Daniel checked his watch. Only a few minutes more until he spoke. He reviewed the sermon he had prepared, looked upward, and said a silent prayer. "Please God, give me the right words."

At eleven A.M. the Torah was returned to the ark, and Daniel mounted the podium. He felt the scrutiny of the larger-than-normal Shabbat morning crowd. Almost every seat in the sanctuary was filled. It was the sermon title, he knew, that had attracted so many. Tell middle-aged Jews you're speaking about children, and they come.

"Shabbat Shalom," he greeted the assemblage, and here and there, a scattering of voices replied. His eyes sought out Janet Karp and then her father, and he nodded, ever so slightly.

"Next to Moses," he began, "perhaps the greatest of the prophets is Elijah. According to Jewish tradition, it is Elijah who is present at every circumcision, and he who visits every Passover seder. When the rabbis of the Talmud encountered a problem too difficult to solve, they declared, 'Someday Elijah will come and solve it.' Elijah is indeed the miracle man of the Jewish tradition—the prophet who is not limited by distances or difficulties. And someday Elijah will perform his greatest task and announce the coming of the Messiah.

"But before the Messiah can come, the Bible tells us, there is one miracle Elijah must perform, a miracle greater than any of his earlier ones. And what is that?" Daniel let the question hang dramatically for a moment. When he resumed, his deep voice was pitched several keys lower. "He shall reconcile fathers with their sons and sons with their fathers."

A sob, barely audible, broke the stillness in the synagogue.

"What makes this task so difficult?

"It is difficult because inherent to the parent-child relationship is conflict and tension.

"A hundred years ago, Oscar Wilde said: 'Children begin by loving their parents. After a time they judge them. Rarely, if ever, do they forgive them.'

"Perhaps Wilde overstated the case. But nonetheless he penetrated to a powerful truth, a truth which the Torah understood thousands of years ago. Children feel love for their parents, yes, but there are times when they feel other emotions as well. And perhaps that is why the Bible commanded that we love God, and our neighbor, and even the stranger, but it did not command that we love our parents. In so intimate a relationship, love is too volatile an emotion to be commanded. The fifth of the Ten Commandments, therefore, demands a standard of honor and respect, a standard that has to go on even when a child is estranged from his parents.

"In the middle of family disagreements it is this honor and respect that children and parents often lose sight of. Recently, a woman told me that she and her husband could not forgive their daughter for a hurt the girl had inflicted upon them." Daniel looked straight ahead. 'Would you make peace with your daughter?' I asked her. 'No.' 'And if your daughter died,' I went on, 'would you feel bad?' 'Yes,' she conceded. 'And would you go to the funeral?' 'Yes.'

"And then I said to her: 'So what are you waiting for before you make peace? For your daughter to die?'"

He did not look at Janet and Milton, but as if by a sixth sense, he knew they were focusing on his words. He saw that the eyes of many of the people seated around were very bright.

"And what are we waiting for," he shouted, "before we're willing to make peace? A great rabbi once said to a Jewish congregation—you're angry at non-Jews for the way they treat Jews, but do you treat Jews so much better? And we? How can we enter God's house and ask for God's mercy, when we show no mercy ourselves?"

Abruptly, he went over to his seat and sat down. The

cantor arose, chanting the kaddish, the Aramaic hymn that precedes the long and silent amidah prayer. But there was little evidence of silence in the congregation. Small knots of people whispered among themselves. Daniel sensed many glances in his direction. "An eloquent speech," he overheard, "but such anger and intensity at the end!" Daniel's heart beat rapidly in his chest. Had his words gotten through?

For the second time that morning, he offered a silent prayer.

Forty-five minutes later, the service ended. Daniel was surrounded. "Powerful sermon, Rabbi," synagogue vice-president Abe Nussbaum declared, and others nodded in assent. Sara Benjamin, eighty-nine years old, her face a map of wrinkles, planted a large wet kiss on his cheek. Daniel acknowledged all the "Gut Shabbos" greetings, but his eyes were directed elsewhere. Near the back of the congregation he caught sight of them, Milton and Janet, eyeing each other and keeping at a distance. Then, with slow steps, Janet walked over to her father. Tentatively, painfully, his face dark with emotion, Karp stretched out his hand to her in the traditional Sabbath manner. Daniel saw her hesitate, and then, with a sudden movement, she threw her arms around her father's neck. "You crying, Rabbi?" Wilbur Kantor asked him, curiously.

He waited a while, stopping to talk to some people, and then he started over to them. Janet and Milton were seated together on the synagogue seats by the far window, alone. Most of the congregation had drifted off. Janet's arm rested on her father's. Neither spoke a word, but their faces glowed. They were hardly conscious of Daniel's approach.

"Gut Shabbos." Daniel put out his hand.

"Do you always tailor-make your sermons like that?" Milton Karp said gruffly, returning the rabbi's handshake.

Daniel smiled. With an apology to Janet, he drew Milton aside.

"I'm very grateful to you, Rabbi."

"I'm very happy," Daniel said. "I really am. Now I need a small favor."

"Name it."

"I need to know what happened that night."

Karp frowned instinctively.

"You did meet with Myra, didn't you?"

Reluctantly, Karp nodded.

"Milton, there's no danger now. But it's important that you tell me when and where you met with her."

"It was like you said," Karp said in a low voice. "I went to find her after the radio show. I knew the route she'd have to take to her house, so I drove until I spotted her. Then I drew up alongside. She stopped and I got out of the car and we talked. It looked like we'd be able to work out something. She'd leave quietly, and I'd personally make sure she got good references. Given the circumstances," Karp laughed mirthlessly, "the discussion was almost amicable."

"And when you left her, did you notice if you were followed?"

"No. But that doesn't mean much, I'm not the sort who would notice something like that."

"And you drove straight home?"

"Yes."

"How long did that take?"

"Three minutes, four minutes maximum."

"Let me ask you, do you have any idea how your next-door neighbor's car came to be stolen?"

Karp shifted his feet.

"Look, Mr. Karp, we now know it wasn't Janet. Do you have any idea who else it might have been?"

Karp shook his head.

"What make of car do you drive?"

"Mercedes."

"Would your car be easy to steal?"

"Fat chance." Karp said vigorously. "I've got a device that shuts down the gas and ignition and seals the hood shut. The thief hasn't been born who could get away with my car."

Daniel nodded pensively, shook Karp's hand in a distracted manner, and strode off. A moment later, as if by instinct, he swung around. Milton Karp was staring after him, looking strangely anxious.

Saturday Night

Daniel dropped the plain gold band into Daryl Kelman's hand. "Put it on Marcia's first finger," he instructed Daryl quietly.

Solemnly, the young man complied. "*Haray aht,*" Daniel prompted, and Daryl followed, "*Haray aht*—you are hereby sanctified unto me with this ring according to the laws of Moses and Israel."

A bridesmaid in a peach-colored gown, wearing a headband of pink roses, handed Marcia a matching ring, which she slipped on Daryl's finger. "I am my beloved's and my beloved is mine," she said, in a clear sweet voice.

Daniel smiled at both of them. "Six months ago," he began, raising his voice so that those gathered could hear, "I met the two of you for the first time. We spoke and I was honored that you asked me to perform your wedding. There was one question, though, that I asked you that day. Do you remember?"

Daryl shook his head, and Marcia smiled, her face shining behind the frail white lace of her veil.

"I asked you each what it was that you particularly loved about the other. You said, Marcia, that it was Daryl's integrity. 'He's an honest man in every way, emotionally, financially, and intellectually. He makes me a better person.' And you, Daryl, said, 'When I'm with Marcia, I'm happy. Happier than I've even been. You know why? Because Marcia believes in me. She knows who I am and loves me anyway.'"

A few laughs punctuated the silence. Standing beside Marcia, her mother sniffled and fumbled for a handkerchief.

163

"Two thousand years ago," Daniel resumed, "it was the custom in ancient Israel that a cedar tree was planted when a boy was born and a cypress tree was planted when a girl was born. When they grew up and married, their wedding canopy was made of branches woven from both trees.

"Tonight, the canopy under which we stand is not woven from such romantic materials." He looked at the plain white canopy under which the couple stood. "But that ancient Jewish tradition teaches us something very profound. When a couple marry, their relationship is woven together from the experiences and wisdom they're acquired since they were born." He paused and studied their young faces. "Your integrity, Daryl, your emotional balance and happiness, Marcia." He let his glance linger on Marcia and prayed that what he said was true for Daryl, too. "When two people as fine as yourselves come together, it is indeed a time for rejoicing."

Daniel read aloud the ketubah, the marriage document, and then made the seven final blessings. A glass had been prepared on a small table, and now Daniel raised it, then placed it by Daryl's foot. "According to Jewish tradition," he explained to the guests, "at a time of great joy, we break something valuable to remind ourselves that we are living in an unredeemed world." He looked from Marcia to Daryl. "May the children of your union help bring about this world's redemption."

Daryl brought his foot down on the glass and shattered it. Instantly, a hundred voices cried, "Mazal tov!" Guests streamed over to embrace the young couple. With some difficulty, Daniel ushered them across the synagogue hall.

"One final law," he told the couple, as he shepherded them into his office. "After the ceremony you have to be alone for at least ten minutes. Although," he added, looking at their faces, "I'm sure you won't find that too hard."

Daniel stood guard outside with the cantor, and together they fended off the photographer. At the end of ten minutes, Daniel rapped on the door.

"Come in," Marcia Diskin Kelman called out. She rushed over to him, her long dress trailing gracefully behind. "Rabbi, thank you. It was wonderful."

"And you, Daryl," he asked, noting the groom's unusual silence. "What did you think of it?"

Kelman's cheeks were red. "I apologize for last week, Rabbi."

"No need, no need."

"But I do, Rabbi. I have to tell you something. As you led us out of the hall just now, the dean of the college grabbed me for a second and you know what he said?" Marcia squeezed his hand, her face radiant. "He said that this was the most beautiful service he'd ever attended."

Marcia brought out a package.

"We have something for you, Rabbi." Daniel looked down at the elaborate green wrapping. "Remember what I told you last week, that I taped every show of *Religion and You*?" She carefully unwound the wrapping, exposing an elegant leather attaché case. She flipped it open. Inside were compartments filled with cassettes. "Well, here's the last year of your show."

A moment later, the relentless photographer burst in and pulled the young couple out. Daniel was left alone in his office. Absently, he started to pull the tapes out. Marcia Diskin had dated every one of them. Soon he located the one he wanted. He knew he should go back and join the wedding party for the dinner, but suddenly he had no desire to. *They don't need me there, anyway,* he told himself. He sat down at his desk and inserted the most recent cassette into his recorder. For a few seconds he heard a whirring sound and then his own voice. It sounded high, even a little scratchy. *That's not what I sound like,* he thought, with a slight embarrassment. Then came the introductions, and his attention was jolted back. "Rabbi Wahl is . . . sitting here in a green jogging suit, and tells us she will be jogging home after the show." Remembering his conversation with Milton Karp, he winced. He had announced Myra's whereabouts to two hundred and fifty thousand people. And one of them had killed her.

He listened straight through for over an hour. Then suddenly he depressed the stop switch. For a few moments he sat at his desk, hands locked together, staring at the wall opposite him. He turned back to his tape machine, pushed down rewind, and let it run a few seconds. Then he replayed the last section.

His heart racing, he picked up his telephone and dialed information. "Myra Wahl, please," he said, and spelled the name. "I'm also going to want some more information," he added, before the operator could activate the computerized voice.

"I'll stay on the line," the woman said. She read off Myra Wahl's number.

"Do you have an address on that?" Daniel asked.

"1906 Lincoln."

"I also need information on Joanne Short, in West Los Angeles, please."

The number was given to him.

"I want to make sure it's the right Short," he said. "Do you have an address on that?"

"10826 Brooke," the operator answered.

Odd that their addresses were both listed, he thought. But maybe not so odd. They were both feminists. Tough. Unafraid.

He pulled out his battered blue telephone book. A moment later he was speaking to Rabbi Reuben Rappaport.

"*Gut vokh*, Reuben," he said.

"And a good week to you, Daniel," Rappaport replied. "I hear my president went slumming in your synagogue today."

Daniel explained briefly that he had needed to talk to Milton Karp.

"But let me tell you why I'm calling, Reuben. There's a little thing I needed to know. Did Myra Wahl have a secretary?"

"Yes. Debbie. Debbie Berkowitz."

"I need to speak with her."

"No problem. Call the temple Monday morning."

"I need to speak with her right now. Do you have her number with you?"

"Wait a minute," Rappaport said, obviously startled at Daniel's urgency. Soon he was back. "I have a sheet here with our employees' home phones. I just hope it's up to date."

Daniel scribbled the number on the back of an old phone message.

He called. Six rings. No answer. Frustrated, he banged the receiver down and started pacing his office. Five long minutes later he dialed again. Nothing. He wandered out of the office. Downstairs, a band struck up the hora. A young boy in a dark velvet suit, his white frilled shirt spotted with what looked like juice, rushed out into the hall, exultant at having apparently escaped from a posse of other children.

"You're the rabbi, aren't you?" he demanded, breathing hard.

"Yes."

"My name is David Parednick." The boy stuck out a hand, which had seen cleaner evenings, a mischievous grin on his elfin face. Solemnly Daniel shook it. "My mom says rabbis are very smart. Are you?"

"I like to think so."

"Then I'm gonna ask you a riddle."

"Okay."

"Spell the word 'spot.'"

"S-P-O-T."

"Pronounce the word 'spot.'"

"Spot."

"What do you do at a green light?"

"Stop."

"No, Rabbi, you *go* at a green light," the boy said, doubling over with laughter. Daniel thought for a second, then joined in.

A few minutes later, when he waved good-bye and went back to his office, he found himself mulling over the boy's riddle. Once again, he dialed Debbie Berkowitz's number. On the fifth ring, a breathless voices answered.

He was barely able to suppress the excitement in his voice. "Is this Debbie Berkowitz?"

"Yes," she said, struggling to catch her breath. "I literally this second got home from Mexico. Let me set down my suitcases."

He waited with mounting impatience till she returned. Then he identified himself and asked her one question. "No," she answered firmly. He was about to hang up when she spoke again.

"It's the oddest thing, Rabbi."

"What?"

"Wednesday afternoon, Reverend Joanne Short called me at the temple, insisting she needed to speak to me. But when I got to her house, all she asked me was one question."

"Oh, and what was that?"

"The same one you just asked."

His next call was to Brenda. Her answering hello, was shaky.

"Are you okay?"

"To tell you the truth, Daniel, I feel like I'm going mad. For the first time, we're really on the trail of my parents' murderer. And yet it's so frustrating. You saw what happened last night: the more we go over what we know, the more nothing fits. We're like kids with a jigsaw puzzle piece that doesn't go in anywhere. It's driving me crazy."

"Brenda, I know how to make the piece fit."

"What are you talking about?"

"I know who murdered your parents. And Myra Wahl and Joanne Short."

"How could you know?"

"Trust me. I do. That's why we've got to talk, you, me, and Cerezzi. Immediately."

"Wait. Stay right where you are. Don't do *anything* . . . don't move. I'll call Joe and get back to you this instant."

After they hung up, Daniel paced the room uneasily, alert for any sound. Now that he had solved the riddle of the murders, he started imagining that the murderer knew that he knew. Crazy, he thought. But he jumped when he heard a bang just outside his office door, and instinctively snatched up the scissors on his desk. Then he looked out the window and laughed ruefully. A departing wedding guest had knocked over a garbage can.

Seconds later, the ringing telephone set his blood racing. He grabbed it, almost knocking over his chair.

"I spoke to Joe," Brenda said in a breathless, strained voice. "Be at my house in fifteen minutes."

Cerezzi relaxed into the soft white armchair in Brenda Goldstein's living room and eased his big body back. He nodded at Brenda and then turned to Daniel, "Shoot, Rabbi."

"I have a riddle for you."

"Come again?"

"I heard a riddle tonight. I want to try it on you."

Cerezzi looked at Brenda, one eye cocked. "He's serious, right?"

She nodded.

"Okay," he turned back to Daniel, wearily. The stress of the past six days was etched on his face. "What's the riddle?"

"First, spell the word 'spot.'"

"S-P-O-T."

"Now pronounce it."

"Spot."

"What do you do at a green light?"

"Stop," said Cerezzi, and shot an irritable look at Brenda, who sat on the edge of the sofa, her hands clenched, her face pale.

"No, Lieutenant. You *go* at a green light."

Cerezzi had the grace to chuckle softly. "Gonna try that one out on Captain Grier. I bet he'll fall for it. Come on, Rabbi, you didn't bring me out here at midnight to tell me riddles."

"Lieutenant, that riddle helped me figure out who the murderer is.

"I asked you a moment ago what you do at a green light, and you said stop. An absurd answer, right? No offense, Lieutenant. I gave the same answer. Why did we both make that?" Although his eyes were on Cerezzi, Daniel was acutely conscious of Brenda's intense silence. "Because we *assumed* the riddle's purpose was to confuse us between 'spot' and 'stop.' That was our first error. Because we started with a wrong assumption, we were led to a wrong conclusion. Well, that's what's happened in this case. We assumed that Myra Wahl was murdered by someone who knew her, and so the whole investigation has focused on the people who were known to have disagreements with Myra: Karp, because she had dangerous information about his past, and—er—the woman who wrote Myra that note, the phone call that threatened Myra and Joanne Short and for that matter, me. As a result, we overlooked all the people who didn't know Myra."

"But, Rabbi, we've already established that Myra Wahl's death was no accident. The murderer stole that car and aimed it straight at her." Cerezzi glowered. "Are you seriously suggesting that our murderer killed someone he'd never *met*?"

"Yes."

"Why?"

"Because," Daniel went on deliberately, "he had a very definite grievance against Myra Wahl."

"For God's sake, what?"

"That's exactly what I'm getting to." Daniel told them briefly about the tapes Marcia Kelman had given him that evening. "As I listened to Sunday's show, a few things struck me. First, thousands of people heard me announce that Myra Wahl was wearing a green jogging suit and would be running home. Any one of them could have shown up at KLAX in his car and recognized Myra, even if he'd never met—"

"But why?" Cerezzi snapped.

"That's my second point." Daniel explained about the Scrambler and then took out the tape recorder he had brought along and played Laura's call. Brenda strained forward, listening attentively; Cerezzi looked skeptically at the ceiling, rubbing his forehead. Abruptly, Daniel stopped the machine. "So here was a woman," he said, "giving us a false name, telling us that her husband had been in jail, but that she knew he was guilty of something much worse than the crime he had been imprisoned for. Imagine if her husband had heard such a call."

For the first time, Brenda spoke. "I thought you said the Scrambler makes the speaker unrecognizable."

"That's what I thought," Daniel replied. "Until I used it again on Tuesday's show. A guy called up, and inside of thirty seconds I recognized him as a member of my congregation, Eddie Schwartz. You know why? Because he said 'raison d'être' and 'ergo.' Schwartz never speaks without using those words. It suddenly occurred to me that a lot more than the timbre of a voice makes an unseen person recognizable. You see, Laura gave us a false name and her voice was disguised. She might even have deliberately mixed up a few facts. But she couldn't alter them entirely, could she? After all, the whole reason she was calling was to get help, and to do that she had to at least hint at the truth. Which is why I'm convinced that the major detail she did give us, that her husband had committed a far more serious crime than the one that sent him to jail, is true."

"So what do we do now?" Cerezzi asked. "Investigate everyone who's been in prison for under two years? Do you have any idea of how many people we'd be checking?"

"Stay with me, Lieutenant." Again Daniel turned to the tape recorder, "Now both of you listen to this." He pressed down the play button, and immediately Myra Wahl's voice came on. "Don't worry, Laura, I'll see you first thing tomorrow morning." Daniel stopped the machine. "If Laura's husband heard Myra say that, doesn't it make sense that he'd try and stop that meeting from taking place?"

"Christ! You know, Rabbi, you might be on to something there. But how do we figure out who Laura is?"

"That's the easy part, Lieutenant. Laura was the other woman killed Sunday night. And Laura's husband is the man I met in your office, Elmer Brine."

"How could you know that?" Brenda stammered.

"Just bear with me a few more minutes. Myra Wahl's death, if you recall, was not announced by the media till late Monday morning."

"That's right," Cerezzi said. His dark eyes glowed with excitement. "We didn't release the name till the family had been notified."

"Even so," Daniel said, moving to Brenda's side, "a few people knew about it earlier. I, for example, heard of it from Brenda. Milton Karp learned of it from Rabbi Rappaport, who, I understand, was notified by one of your people."

"We called him to locate Myra's parents."

"But presumably almost no one else knew. Including

Laura. Which means that she had every reason to show up early Monday morning for her appointment with Myra." He took a breath. "Two hours ago, I spoke to Myra Wahl's secretary. I asked her one question. On Monday morning did a woman, giving the name Laura or any other name, show up for a meeting with Rabbi Wahl? Her answer was no."

"That's not exactly definitive, Rabbi. Laura might have panicked or settled things with her husband—who knows, a million things."

"Debbie Berkowitz also told me one other fact. On Wednesday afternoon, someone else asked her the same question I did—"

"Joanne Short," Brenda whispered, her trembling hands on her face.

Daniel nodded, squeezing her shoulder.

"Anyway, we'll come back to that in a minute. In the meantime, Lieutenant, let me ask you one final question. What was Elmer Brine in prison for?" Daniel knew the answer. He had read Elmer Brine's file in Brenda's office on Thursday, but he had no desire to own up to this.

"He was a car thief," Cerezzi said, his voice husky.

"Exactly. Now let me tell you what really happened.

"Somehow, Elaine Brine discovered that her husband was a murderer." He looked into Brenda's stricken eyes and said softly, "With what we've learned about the gun that killed Joanne Short, I would guess that he was the one who killed your parents. This is what Elaine Brine somehow learned. Elaine Brine called up *Religion and You* on Sunday night because she was terrified and desperately needed to talk. What better listeners than three clergy? Unfortunately—and I don't feel good about this at all—she trusted the scrambler to hide her identity. Somewhere, the only person for whom her words would have any significance was listening. Elmer Brine realized that his wife was scared enough to turn him in. He must have decided that the only way to silence her was to murder her. Perhaps he killed her accidentally, trying to convince her not to betray him. He arrogantly assumed he could disguise her death as the result of a break-in, Brenda. But then, to his horror, he realized there was one other person who'd now have reason to suspect him—Myra Wahl. She had set up a meeting with Elaine Brine. Who knows what else Elaine might have already told Myra in that private conversation they had in the studio? Maybe her name, maybe what her husband had done. He couldn't be sure. And even if she had only arranged to see Myra, he knew Myra would become suspicious if after such a panicky call 'Laura' didn't show up the next morning. It wouldn't be hard for her to make the connection between the woman murdered Sunday night, Elaine Brine, and Laura. So, after strangling his wife, Elmer Brine decided Myra had to die, too. Because of my stupid announcement on the air, he knew not only what Myra looked like, but that she would be jogging home. That's why it was so easy for him to find her."

"Go on," the lieutenant said softly.

"Brine drove to KLAX and watched Myra start her run. Only, before he could act, another car came and cut her off. You know, of course, who was in that car?"

"Karp," Cerezzi said. "He told us the whole story."

"Brine followed Myra. He saw Karp stop her and he watched them talk. When Karp pulled away, Brine decided to follow Karp."

"Why?"

"Because he'd suddenly found a way to pin Myra's murder on someone else. He figured that he'd follow Karp home, steal his car, and—"

"Hold it, Rabbi," the lieutenant gestured with his hand. "You just lost me. If Brine—assuming he's the killer—took off after Karp, how did he know he'd find Myra again?"

"No problem. Even if he didn't run her down, as he had planned, he knew where she lived."

Daniel walked over to the telephone next to Cerezzi's chair and held out the receiver. "Dial 411 and you can learn Myra Wahl's address, too. Joanne Short's also, for that matter."

Cerezzi set the receiver back in its cradle.

"Elmer Brine knew where Myra lived. When Karp drove off, Brine realized it would be a full half hour before Myra would get home. He decided to take a desperate gamble. If he could steal Milton Karp's car in time, he'd run her down. And if not, he'd break into her apartment and shoot her. He did have experience doing that, you know."

Brenda's body stiffened.

"But he didn't steal Karp's car?" Cerezzi protested.

"He couldn't. And I found out why. Karp's Mercedes is burglarproof. He's quite proud of it. When he locks up his car, the ignition shuts off, the hood locks, and only he can restart it."

Cerezzi nodded. "I know that device. Bit of a nuisance, but he's right. No burglar can get into it."

"Anyway, Brine followed him home, and when Karp went inside, he tried breaking into the Mercedes. No luck. In desperation, he spotted the car next door. Not as good as using Karp's, but infinitely less incriminating than using his own." Daniel paused. "Tell me something, Lieutenant. How long would it take an experienced car thief to break into a car and drive off?"

"Under a minute," Cerezzi said grimly.

Daniel nodded. "So he stole the car, used it to kill Myra, and then brought it back. When Milton Karp was arrested, Brine must have had a good laugh. That is, until he found out Joanne Short suspected him."

"How did she figure that, Rabbi?"

"Because Joanne Short was twice as smart as any of us. On Wednesday, she spoke to Debbie Berkowitz and confirmed that 'Laura' hadn't shown up to see Myra on Monday. On Thursday morning, she went scouting around for Monday's newspapers. Why? To find out who else died Sunday night. It fits, Lieutenant. A short time after she got the Monday paper, she phoned you to say she knew who the murderer was."

"How did Brine know she had called me?"

Daniel shrugged. "When we catch him, we'll get the answer to that one. In the meantime, if I may, I could venture a guess."

Cerezzi's grin was lopsided. "You've never asked permission before. No reason to start now."

"For some reason, Joanne Short must have telephoned Brine. Perhaps to test her theory or to put a scare into him. I don't know. We'll probably never know for sure. But I'm convinced that's what happened."

"Even so, Rabbi, she wouldn't have told him her name."

"She didn't have to."

"What do you mean?"

"When I met Brine at your office, all I said to him was hello, and he said to me, 'You're Daniel Winter.'" I remember being puzzled that he recognized me on the basis of one word, and he told me he had this gift. If he hears a voice, he never forgets it. Remember, on Sunday night he heard Joanne Short on *Religion and You*. She didn't realize it, of course, when she called him, but he knew immediately who she was. It was a simple matter for him to get her address from information."

For a few minutes, the only sound in the room was their breathing.

"It's just so sad," Brenda whispered. "We've been running around the whole week thinking Myra died because of an argument. Now we find she was murdered because she heard a woman in pain and tried to help her."

Cerezzi was hardly listening. Distractedly, he tapped his fingers on the table, and finally he shook his head.

"Ingenious, Rabbi, and quite incredible. But you realize, of course, that all your evidence is purely circumstantial."

"What does that mean, Lieutenant?" Brenda's voice was icy. "That Brine's going to get away? Again?"

Cerezzi stared at Daniel and his eyes narrowed.

"I need your help, Rabbi. I have an idea I want to try out. If all goes well, I'm pretty sure it will work."

Daniel took Brenda's hand and squeezed it.

"It better work," he said.

Sunday Morning

"Mr. Brine? This is Daniel Winter. We met at Lieutenant Cerezzi's office."

"Of course." Brine's voice was smoothly deferential. "I'm honored to hear from you. Radio stars don't usually call me."

Daniel laughed politely.

"As a matter of fact, I'm calling with some good news for you."

"What do you mean?"

"Remember what you told me when we met? That Cerezzi was harassing you, treating you as a suspect."

"Yes?" The voice turned suddenly cautious.

"Well, I know for a fact that you're not under suspicion anymore."

"How do you know that?"

"Early this morning, I was at Cerezzi's office, in the waiting room—you know, where we met. Inside, Cerezzi was briefing some cops, and I overheard him explain some new developments in the case. Apparently, the police now have reason to believe that your wife was murdered by the same person who killed Rabbi Wahl, Reverend Short, and maybe somebody else. So that clears you."

Silence.

"One thing more." Daniel's voice grew excited. "And this is the clincher."

"What?"

"Your wife's name was Elaine. Right?"

"Yes."

"Well, somehow the police know the name of the

murderer's wife, and it's not Elaine." Daniel paused. "It's Laurie or Laura."

Brine said nothing.

"So I guess that means you're off the hook," Daniel said sympathetically. "Knowing how upset you were on Tuesday, I'm happy I could give you this news."

"Yeah . . . well, thanks."

Daniel hung up, and Cerezzi put down the extension in the adjoining room, walked back in, and flashed a thumbs up. "Beautiful, Rabbi. A born actor. That should do it. We'll know very soon if he's our man. After this call, I predict Brine will be inside of his car in half an hour."

"But what good does that do us, Lieutenant?" Brenda said impatiently. "Our case is still circumstantial."

"Listen. Brine was paroled after serving only one-and-a-half years of a three-year burglary sentence. As a parolee he can't leave California without permission from his parole officer. The moment he does, we have the right to pick him up. Don't worry, Brenda. When we do, we'll get the truth. Now that we know what we're looking for, we'll find it." He saw the dissatisfaction on both their faces. "Look, relax, the two of you. All we have to do now is wait."

Daniel invited them into his kitchen. He made two cups of strong coffee and toasted some bagels. Cerezzi took his coffee, spread a liberal portion of cream cheese on his bagel, and ate it hungrily. Brenda ignored the food and sat sipping her coffee, her hands gripping the edges of the cup, her face very white. Daniel puttered, making more messes than he cleaned up, stopping occasionally to run a hand through his hair.

It was an eternal forty minutes. When at last the phone rang, Daniel raced over to it. "For you," he said, handing the receiver to Cerezzi.

Brenda and Daniel listened tensely, but Cerezzi confined his responses to monosyllables. When he put the phone down, though, his smile was broad.

"Brine just got into his car and took off. He packed two suitcases in the trunk. As of this moment, Elmer Brine is finished."

Monday Morning

Daniel sat at his desk, studying the front-page photograph in the *Times*. It showed a grim-faced Lieutenant Joseph Cerezzi bringing in stooped and handcuffed "murder suspect" Elmer Brine. The article told of Brine's arrest at the Mexican border. The arresting officer had found a gun on him. Ballistics quickly identified it as the murder weapon in the deaths of Joanne Short and Ted and Jean Kaplan. With this evidence in hand, Cerezzi had secured a search warrant. Minutes later, some of Jean Kaplan's jewelry had been found in Brine's suitcase.

Daniel finished the article for the third time and laid the newspaper down. He looked again at the pink slip Pat had given him when he arrived that morning. "Bartley Turner needs to hear from you IMMEDIATELY." He picked up his phone and dialed slowly. Seconds later he was speaking to Turner, who was as jovial as usual.

"What's the story, Danny boy? Are we in business?"

"Bartley, I'm going to stay a rabbi."

Turner groaned dramatically. "Do you realize what you're throwing away?"

"That works two ways, Bartley."

"Which means?"

"If I leave the rabbinate, I'm throwing away a lot, too."

"How can you compare the two things—when was the last time you had half a million—maybe a million—people at one of your services?"

"You're right, Bartley," Daniel said. "The two jobs can't be compared." He thought fleetingly of the reconciliation between Janet and Milton Karp, of the wedding of Marcia and Daryl Kelman, of the bar mitzvah student who had returned the watch. Somehow, he couldn't imagine those things happening if he were a talk-show host. "You know something, Bartley," he said, "it's hard being a rabbi—"

"So?" Turner interrupted.

"But it's worth it. And it's what I want to do. . . . Can you understand that?"

"It's your choice," Turner said, with reluctance. "But I think you're making a big mistake."

Daniel hung up and sat at his desk, brooding. Fifteen minutes later, his phone rang.

"Daniel," Pat said, her voice harsh with urgency. "Come out here immediately. There's an emergency."

He rushed out of his office, banging his knee as he moved around the corner of his desk.

Halfway through the door, hand on his injured knee, he was halted by shouts of "Surprise!"

The entire synagogue staff was there, Pat Hastings, Luther Johnson, the cantor, and the others. Even Wilbur Kantor had come, bringing most of the board of directors with him. The Karps were there, too. And to Daniel's delight he spotted Brenda, Joe Cerezzi at her side. Pat's desk had been converted to a mini banquet table, crowned by an enormous chocolate cake. The vanilla icing inscription read: "To Rabbi Daniel Winter—Detective."

"Mazal tov," Luther Johnson led the first toast, and then Daniel found himself surrounded by a crush of well-wishers. Looking around at the exuberant gathering, a lump rose in his throat. At that moment he was sure, as sure as a man can be of anything in this world. Bartley Turner could think what he wanted. But he knew. He had not made a mistake.

Daniel did not remember much about the party, except that it seemed to be over very fast. Brenda stayed behind after everyone else had left.

"It's finally over," she said, collapsing into the armchair in Daniel's office.

Daniel nodded. He felt a little dazed. But very happy. "You know," Brenda went on. "I feel strange. It hasn't fully registered that this nightmare is over. For two years now, one thing has obsessed me—catching the man who murdered my parents." She paused and then smiled. "Now I'm ready to start something new."

"Like what?"

Rising, she walked over to Daniel and pulled him up gently from his chair. She kissed him full on the mouth, a long, firm, tender kiss. For the briefest moment Daniel resisted, but he knew he didn't want to. In the end, it was Brenda who broke away.

"You know," Daniel said, finally. "I think it's time we got to know each other better. Do you agree?"

"*I do*," she said.

ABOUT THE AUTHOR

JOSEPH TELUSHKIN was ordained a rabbi by Yeshiva University and is now completing a doctorate in Jewish history at Columbia University. He is currently a Fellow at Hebrew University, residing in Jerusalem. He is the co-author of *Why the Jews?* and *The Nine Questions People Ask About Judaism*.

☐ 25789-7 **JUST ANOTHER DAY IN PARADISE,**
Maxwell $2.95

Fiddler has more money than he knows what to do with, he's tried about everything he'd ever thought of trying and there's not much left that interests him. So, when his ex-wife's twin brother disappears, when the feds begin to investigate the high-tech computer company the twin owns, and when Fiddler finds himself holding an envelope of Russian-cut diamonds, he decides to get involved. Is his ex-wife's twin selling high-tech information to the Russians?

☐ 26201-7 **NOT TILL A HOT JANUARY,**
Adamson $2.95

Introducing New York Homicide Detective Balthazar Marten. Balthazar Marten finds himself on special assignment in San Juan, Puerto Rico, far from the cold New York streets. Things really heat up when three coeds are strangled and Marten finds himself on the trail of a psycho.

☐ 25717-X **THE BACK-DOOR MAN,** Kantner $2.95

Ben Perkins doesn't look for trouble, but he isn't the kind of guy who looks the other way when something comes along to spark his interest. In this case, it's a wealthy widow who's a victim of embezzlement and the gold American Express card she gives him for expenses. Ben thinks it should be fun; the other people after the missing money are out to change his mind.

☐ 26061-8 **"B" IS FOR BURGLAR,** Grafton $3.50

"Kinsey is a refreshing heroine."—*Washington Post Book World*

"Kinsey Millhone . . . is a stand-out specimen of the new female operatives."   —*Philadelphia Inquirer*

[Millhone is] "a tough cookie with a soft center, a gregarious loner."   —*Newsweek*

What appears to be a routine missing persons case for private detective Kinsey Millhone turns into a dark tangle of arson, theft and murder.

Look for them at your bookstore or use the coupon below:

BANTAM
SHOP·AT·HOME
C·A·T·A·L·O·G

Special Offer
Buy a Bantam Book
for only 50¢.

Now you can have Bantam's catalog filled with hundreds of titles plus take advantage of our unique and exciting bonus book offer. A special offer which gives you the opportunity to purchase a Bantam book for only 50¢. Here's how!

By ordering any five books at the regular price per order, you can also choose any other single book listed (up to a $4.95 value) for just 50¢. Some restrictions do apply, but for further details why not send for Bantam's catalog of titles today!

Just send us your name and address and we will send you a catalog!